2010

DATE DUE

OCT 2 2012			

Demco, Inc. 38-293

THE HISTORICAL HOUSE

This series is a unique collaboration between three
award-winning authors, Adèle Geras, Linda Newbery
and Ann Turnbull, all writing about one very special
house and the extraordinary young women
who have lived there throughout history.

The Historical House

Adèle Geras
Lizzie's Wish

Cecily's Portrait

ᛞ

Linda Newbery
Polly's March

Andie's Moon

ᛞ

Ann Turnbull
Josie Under Fire

Mary Ann & Miss Mozart

LINDA NEWBERY

Andie's Moon

USBORNE

McLean County Unit #5
201-EJHS

To Ann and Adèle, with love.
Special thanks to Dorothy Hopkins and to John Liffen of the
Science Museum, and of course to Megan Larkin,
who started it all off.

First published in 2007 by Usborne Publishing Ltd., Usborne House,
83-85 Saffron Hill, London EC1N 8RT, England.
www.usborne.com

Copyright © Linda Newbery, 2007
The right of Linda Newbery to be identified as the author of this work has been
asserted by her in accordance with the Copyright, Designs and Patents Act, 1988.

Cover photography: House © Sarah Perkins. Model © Condé Nast Archive/CORBIS.
Girl © Getty Images (Tony Anderson). Astronaut © NASA Kennedy Space Center
(NASA-KSC).
Inside illustrations by Ian McNee.

The name Usborne and the devices ♀ 🎈 are Trade Marks of Usborne Publishing Ltd.

All rights reserved. No part of this publication may be reproduced, stored in a retrieval
system or transmitted in any form or by any means, electronic, mechanical, photocopying,
recording or otherwise without the prior permission of the publisher.

This is a work of fiction. The characters, incidents, and dialogues are products of the
author's imagination and are not to be construed as real. Any resemblance to actual
events or persons, living or dead, is entirely coincidental.

A CIP catalogue record for this book is available from the British Library.

UK ISBN 9780746073100 · First published in America in 2009.AE
American ISBN 9780794523336

JFMAMJJASON /08   Printed in the UK.

Contents

6 Chelsea Walk, 1969

Basement

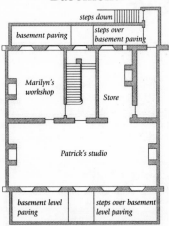

steps down

basement paving

steps over basement paving

Marilyn's workshop

Store

Patrick's studio

basement level paving

steps over basement level paving

First-floor apartment

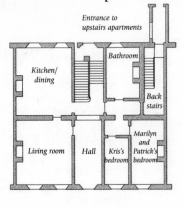

Entrance to upstairs apartments

Kitchen/dining

Bathroom

Back stairs

Living room

Hall

Kris's bedroom

Marilyn and Patrick's bedroom

Second-floor apartment

Kitchen/dining

Bathroom

Back stairs

Stairs up removed

Stairs from below sealed off

Living room

Sushila's bedroom

Ravi's bedroom

Mr. & Mrs. Kapoor's bedroom

Third-floor apartment

Kitchen/dining

Store

Bathroom

Back stairs

Living room

Andie and Prune's bedroom

Mr & Mrs. Miller's bedroom

Roof space

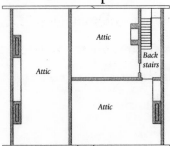

Attic

Attic

Back stairs

Attic

Attic

Chapter One

Fly me to the Moon

Andie didn't know where she was – only that something had woken her, and she was staring into darkness.

She sat up, clutching her pillow. The room came into focus: dark shapes of armoire and chest of drawers; tall, light rectangles of curtained windows. It wasn't her own bedroom, cluttered and square, with its one small window where the street light shone in; this was a much larger space. From the other bed, farthest from the door, came soft steady breathing.

Of course. She was in the Chelsea apartment – this strange new place that seemed so grand and spacious. This was her first night in the room she and Prune were to share, the bedroom that was really Anne Rutherford's. The door to the hall was open, but there were no lights on, so Mum and Dad must have gone to bed too. Andie pounded her pillow into a comfortable hollow, rolled over and settled for sleep – then heard, again, the sound that had got into her dream and woken her. Across the ceiling, directly above her bed, creaked the slow tread of feet.

She sat up and groped for the switch of her bedside lamp.

"Prune!" she called softly. "*Prune!* There's a burglar or something!"

Prune was a heavy sleeper. Andie had to cross the carpet and shake her by the shoulder before she stirred, and by that time the creaking had stopped.

"Wassamatter?" Prune muttered.

"There's someone creeping about!"

"What? Mmm. *You* are." Prune propped herself on one elbow and pushed her hair out of her eyes.

"No, listen! There's someone on the floor above – I heard footsteps."

"Maybe someone lives up there. Or you were dreaming. Go back to sleep."

Rolling over to face the wall, Prune tugged the sheet up to her ears. Andie climbed back into bed, and looked at her watch. Ten past midnight. Not a sound from above now; maybe she'd only imagined the footsteps. She clicked off the lamp, and lay staring up at the high ceiling, wondering what was beyond it.

That man from downstairs, Patrick, who'd shown them around, had said something about attic rooms where servants used to live, but he hadn't mentioned anyone living there *now*. Why would someone be creeping around the attic at midnight?

Andie felt a shiver of excitement run through

her. This was so different from home, which, in comparison to Number Six, Chelsea Walk, seemed very dull – a brick semidetached house, identical to all the others nearby. This house was *old* – built in seventeen hundred and something. Who would even know how many people had lived here, over the years? It had been a big family house, Patrick had told them, before it was divided into apartments. Imagine, one family having this whole huge place to themselves! They must have been incredibly rich. When Andie thought of all the different people who must have walked up and down the stairs and moved through these rooms and slept in the house and breathed its air, she felt dizzy. It was like looking through the wrong end of a telescope, back into history. She was vague about the details, but she imagined a procession of people, their clothes and faces and hair getting more and more old-fashioned, all the way back to seventeen-hundred-and-whatever-it-was. They crowded into her mind, in black-and-white photographs at first, then portraits in oval frames.

Not only did this house have three floors, each one separate apartment, but it had the attic and basement as well – making it, Andie thought, a -story house, really. As soon as Patrick mentioned attic, she'd pictured herself sitting up there with her paints and an easel. She hadn't *got* an easel, but to be the kind of painter who sat in an attic, she'd need to get one somehow. If it was a bit sparse up there, just bare boards, so much the better. That would make her feel like a real artist.

But the noise. The footsteps.

What if something awful had happened here, and someone was prowling about the attic at night, unhappy, or seeking revenge?

No. Andie didn't believe in ghosts. She definitely didn't.

She pushed back the covers and swung her feet to the carpet. Careful not to wake Prune again, she tiptoed to the window and looked out. She could hear traffic, along the Embankment, and over the nearby bridge; through the foliage of the trees that lined Chelsea Walk she saw the glow of street lamps, and, beyond, the glimmer of water that was the River Thames. At home in Slough, in their cul-de-sac, the nights were quiet apart from the odd late car returning home, but Andie supposed that London never slept. There was a hum of busyness, even at this late hour.

And above it all hung the moon, the full moon, cool and silver, the same moon that Andie saw when she looked up from her own garden at home.

Wasn't there a saying, she thought, about it being unlucky to look at the moon through glass? Or was it only looking at the *new* moon through glass? Not wanting to bring bad luck, not on the first night of her stay in London, she opened the window and kneeled on the floor, her elbows on the sill. Now she could gaze as much as she wanted, with the night air fresh on her face.

When she was little, Andie pretended to see the Man in the Moon, because Dad used to tell her a story about him. She liked to imagine that the moon's greeny-blue shadows formed the outline of a face, a wise and good-humored face. The Man, she thought, was smiling at her. He was hard to make out, but perhaps that was why not everyone could see him. He only appeared to especially observant people, and Andie liked to think she was one of those.

Now, everyone was talking about man *on* the moon, because in two weeks' time American astronauts would not only fly to the moon, but land there. Just thinking about it gave Andie a thrill of excitement and disbelief. Did the moon *know*?

"Fly me to the Moon" – that was one of the songs on Mum's favorite Frank Sinatra record. The familiar tune started to sing itself in Andie's head; because of Apollo 11, it was always being played on the radio this summer. Soon, flying to the moon wouldn't be the fantasy it had once been. But, gazing at it now – at *her* moon, the moon she always looked for, and the moon she used to think looked back at her – Andie couldn't quite take in that this was the same place they were aiming for. The moon was Earth's mysterious companion, keeping half of itself always hidden. The space rockets seemed like ropes, lassoes, thrown out to catch and tether it and bring it closer. Apollo 10 had already orbited, with three astronauts aboard, and they'd seen what no human had ever seen before – the far side of the moon.

Mystery, or discovery? Which was better? And could you have *both*?

A moonscape began to form in her mind, sharp, clear and perfect. It was far better than she'd ever be able to achieve with paints and brush; but there it was, demanding to be painted. Tomorrow she'd do it.

She crept back into bed, hearing, as she did so, another small creak from above. Andie froze, listening.

"Prune?" she whispered. "Are you awake?"

But Prune gave no sign of having heard. Andie stayed where she was for a few more moments, ears straining. Then, hearing no more, she gave up, lay down, and closed her eyes firmly.

Chapter Two

Feet on the Ground

Mungojerrie and Rumpelteazer were the main reason for the Miller family's stay at Chelsea Walk. As Andie was the only one who liked cats, she'd been appointed cat-sitter in chief. She didn't mind that. Forking out Kit-e-Kat twice a day, and keeping the litter tray clean, wasn't much to do in return for staying in a luxurious London apartment.

This kitchen was almost twice as big as the one at

home. Everything was white and gleaming. It looked freshly cleaned when they'd arrived, but the first thing Mum had done was get out rubber gloves and scourers and sponges, to wash and disinfect every surface, faucet and drain.

"You don't have to do that!" Dad told her. "The Rutherfords' cleaner comes every Wednesday."

"You never know." Mum sprinkled scouring powder into the sink. "It looks very nice, but who knows what germs are lurking? Especially with those cats shedding fleas and hairs everywhere."

The cats, like the apartment, belonged to the Rutherfords, who were partners in the insurance company Dad had now joined. While Mr. and Mrs. Rutherford, with their daughter Anne, were in Manchester to set up a new branch there, and Dad, with his new job in the King's Road office, wanted to move to London, it solved everyone's problems for the Millers to move into Number Six, Chelsea Walk. The house at home was up for sale, and Andie's parents were looking for a house or apartment in Chelsea. Such a move would mean leaving behind friends, school, everything that was familiar – daunting, but exciting.

Meanwhile, neither Andie nor Prune could quite believe their luck at getting an extra two weeks of summer vacation. For Prune, who had just finished her O-Levels, coming to Chelsea was the perfect reward, the closest thing to heaven. According to *Honey* magazine, which Prune devoured every month from cover to cover, Chelsea was the trendy heart of London, the switched-on scene, the hub of the fashion universe. "Maybe I'll get taken on by a modeling agency!" she had told Andie, at least five times. "There are loads of them in Chelsea. What if I turn out to be the next Twiggy or Jean Shrimpton?"

Andie could have pointed out that both Twiggy and Jean Shrimpton were a lot prettier as well as a lot thinner than Prune, so maybe it was as well that she hadn't been asked for her opinion. But she knew that Prune would be doing a lot of hanging around the King's Road – starting today, most likely. Prune hadn't decided yet what to do in September. Dad wanted her to stay on at school (but *which* school? Hillsden High, back in Slough – or, if they moved house, one near here?), while Mum thought she should take a secretarial course. Prune wasn't enthusiastic about either.

Part of the fun of missing school was to think of all the classes you weren't having. Andie ran through her Friday timetable: Math, Biology, French and English, and finally double Art. She felt a little leap of joy inside, at the thought of not being there.

Art was her least favorite class. It ought to have been the time of the week she most looked forward to, which made it worse that she hated it. There was something so dispiriting about filing into the big, raftered space on the school's top floor, and hearing Miss Temple's brisk, "Sit down, girls." Art with Miss Temple was deadly. She liked the girls to do still-life drawings or portraits of each other, in pencil or in the powder paints that no matter how thickly you mixed them never kept their brightness on the cheap spongy paper that drained everything of life. The paintbrushes were old and scrubby and looked as if generations of schoolgirls had chewed their wooden ends in frustration. Sometimes, Miss Temple experimented with what she called Modern Art, by which she meant looking at Picasso prints and trying to imitate them by drawing things chopped up into chunks, or viewed from strange angles.

"But Modern Art doesn't mean copying someone else, who's been doing it like that for years and years!" Andie objected. "Modern is *new*. Modern is *now*."

Andie and Miss Temple didn't get along at all. Andie liked to do things her own way, which offended Miss Temple. "When you've spent several years at art college, Andrea, maybe you can come back and tell me how to teach. Until then, I strongly recommend that you do as I tell you." And just being in the same room as Miss Temple sent Andie into one of her dark, depressed moods in which nothing seemed worth doing.

On Andie's report card, Miss Temple had written, in her tight, knotty handwriting: *Andrea has considerable talent, but no self-discipline at all.* And a stingy B-, and C- for effort. Andie's friend Barbara, who didn't even *like* Art but managed to turn out neat, boring pictures week after week according to Miss Temple's instructions, got B+ and A-.

"Oh, Andie!" Mum said, reading the report. "You really mustn't be obstinate. I don't like you getting into trouble at school."

Andie only took notice of the "considerable talent" bit. Well, that was something, however grudgingly Miss Temple had squeezed out the words. Going to art college was exactly what she had in mind for herself, but Mum and Dad were going to need an awful lot of persuading. "Anything goes, these days. It's all Pop Art now, isn't it?" That was Dad's view. "You can be as good as you like at drawing and painting, but where'll that get you? People do comic-book cartoons, or pictures of soup cans, and call that Art."

Mum's line was, "It's a nice hobby, painting. You can do it in evening classes or join a group. But you'll never make money at it."

"Money's not the most important thing there is!" Andie protested.

"No, I know. But you try living without it, and you'll realize that it is *quite* important. When it comes to getting a job, you'll do far better to concentrate on math and English. Then you can learn shorthand and typing. I keep telling Prue, a good grounding like that can get you a job almost anywhere."

"Yes, but only boring jobs in offices!"

"Boring, you may think," retorted Mum, "but office jobs pay well. We wouldn't be going to London, if it wasn't for Dad's job. And as soon as we get there, *I'll* be looking for office work as well. If I decided to sit around all day painting pictures, how would we eat?"

Sometimes Andie gave up arguing; sometimes she didn't. Mum was like that, always going on about keeping your feet on the ground and not having your head in the clouds. *Gaze at the moon and fall in the gutter*, that was one of her sayings. An absurd one, Andie thought. Surely, even if you fell over and grazed your knees or twisted your ankle, it'd be better than plodding along *looking* at the gutter, not raising your eyes any higher to see what was shining in the sky? You'd miss the moon altogether, doing that.

Mum could talk as much as she liked about jobs and offices, but nothing was going to make Andie give up her ambition. How could filing and shorthand-typing ever match the excitement of paint and paper and light?

☙

The Rutherfords' two cats were the haughtiest Andie had ever met. The cat she knew best, Ringo, who belonged to Barbara, would have been purring loudly and wrapping himself around her legs. Mungojerrie and Rumpelteazer sat upright in their basket and stared in disdain. *You're ten minutes late,* they might as well have said aloud. *We hope you're not planning to make this a habit.*

Mrs. Rutherford had left a long list of instructions, which Andie had already studied carefully but now read again. The cats were to be fed twice a day, at eight in the morning and six in the evening precisely, always from clean dishes. They liked whole milk served at room temperature, and on Sunday evenings they were to have canned sardines as a treat. Both were large and sleek, with velvet collars. Mungojerrie was black with a white chin and whiskers; Rumpelteazer striped ginger, with a pink nose.

Andie placed the dishes of meat on the cats' special mat, and filled one bowl with water, a second with milk. The rest of today would be free for going out and finding her way around. Later, this evening, the Millers had been invited down to Patrick's apartment to meet everyone who lived in the house.

When the cats had finished picking at their

breakfast of chicken and tuna, and were sitting on the windowsill washing their paws and faces, Andie went to see if Prune was getting up.

She found Prune out of bed, standing by the mirror, turning this way and that. She was wearing a dress Andie hadn't seen before, the color of purple grapes, with a high collar and a very short skirt.

"Hey, is that new?"

"Oh!" Prune turned round, startled. "I thought you were in the bathroom."

"That dress. Is it new? Where did you get it?"

"No, it's, er, not mine." Prune's face flushed red. "I was just trying it on. I found it in a bag on the top shelf of the armoire."

"So it belongs to the Rutherford girl!"

"I was only looking." Prune turned away with a flounce. "I haven't got anything to wear tonight, and I found this groovy dress. I'm only trying it on. Isn't it fab? It's from Biba." She posed for the mirror: bare legs splayed, toes turned in, both arms held out to show the fullness of the sleeves, which were gathered into long buttoned cuffs.

"Yes, it looks great," Andie conceded, "but you can't help yourself to other people's clothes! Anyway, what does it matter? We're only going downstairs to meet people."

"But they're *Chelsea* people. I don't want them thinking I'm a complete square."

"So you'd rather they think you're a thief? They've probably seen Anne Rutherford wearing it. And Mum and Dad know it's not yours. They won't let you."

"Oh, don't be boring!" Lovingly, Prune stroked the jersey fabric over her hips.

"I'm just *saying*."

"Oh well, I'll have to get something in the King's Road," said Prune, cheering up. "All those fantastic shops, just around the corner! There's Just Looking, and Bazaar, and Top Gear, and it's not far to the Chelsea Cobbler and Biba and Bus Stop – oh, I can't wait! We can go today!"

"We?" said Andie, suspicious.

"You will come, won't you?" Prune was unbuttoning the cuffs. "I can't go on my own! If Susan was here, she'd come like a shot. But she's not, so I'll have to make do with you."

"Huh," went Andie. "Well, don't think you're doing me a favor. It's the other way round, if you ask me."

She didn't see why Prune couldn't go alone; Andie certainly didn't want Prune trailing behind her when she went to art galleries. Andie *liked* being on her own, but that, she told herself, was because she was an artist and had an artist's temperament.

"When you're my age," said Prune, "you'll be just as interested in fashion as I am."

"No, I won't. What's the *point* of it? Everyone trying to copy everyone else? All those magazines telling you what you can and can't wear? Why can't you decide for yourself?"

"You just don't understand!"

"What's going on in there?" called Mum from the hallway. "I hope you two aren't arguing already?"

"Nothing!" Hastily, Prune pulled the Biba dress over her head.

In spite of the scorn she exaggerated to annoy Prune, Andie was curious enough about the King's Road to want to see for herself. They had breakfast with Mum, who was dressed in her cream suit, ready to go and sign on with a temp agency.

"I don't know what time I'll be back," she told the girls, "but you've got your key, haven't you, Prue? Don't get lost, and make sure you stay together."

"It's okay, Mum," said Prune. "Andie's twelve, not six. Even if she acts like it sometimes."

"And don't buy anything outrageous," Mum added.

Chapter Three

Moonscape

Andie had been fidgeting by the front window for at least half an hour before Prune emerged from the bedroom, wearing her flowered dress and red sandals, a little crochet bag slung over one shoulder. She had put on makeup; her face was pale, her eyes ringed in black, their lashes thick with mascara.

"About time!" It was a bright, sunshiny day, and Andie was eager to be outside. "I didn't realize you had to do the full works, just to look around a few shops."

"I s'pose you're going just as you are?" Prune glanced disapprovingly at Andie's yellow T-shirt, jeans and sandals.

"What's wrong with it? Anyway, it'll have to do. I'm not changing."

It was less than five minutes' walk to the King's Road, especially at the pace Prune was setting. Prune didn't like walking, but with clothing boutiques ahead of her she was speeding along in high gear.

"Are you sure they'll let us in?" Andie panted, trotting to keep up – her legs were shorter than Prune's.

"Let us in where?"

"To your King's Road. It sounds like a sort of special club, for rich famous beautiful people. They probably don't want dull ordinary people like us. They'll tell us to go somewhere else."

"Don't be daft!" Prune led the way across Flood Street at a brisk trot. "The only thing that makes me look dull and ordinary is having my kid sister with me."

The King's Road, as far as Andie could see, was just an ordinary street with shops on each side, but very busy with traffic and shoppers. There were cafés, some of which had chairs and tables out on the pavement. Prune was trying to look as if she came here all the time, but Andie knew that she was enthralled; it was like walking into the pages of her precious *Honey* magazine. "Oh!" she kept saying. "Look at that! Oh, and see – and let's go in here –" Most of the shops played loud music that thumped out of open doors, so that walking along the pavement felt like passing a succession of parties, each one inviting you in.

Andie couldn't help staring. There was so much to stare *at*. Boys and men with sleek swishy hair and frilled shirts. Girls in thigh-high boots, even on this warm July day. A young man with an Afro and a tapestry vest, no shirt underneath. Tight velvet trousers, wide-brimmed hats, long strings of wooden beads, short short skirts and a few girls in the new maxi length. *Look at me, look at me,* everyone seemed to be signaling. *I'm young, I'm beautiful, I know what to buy and what to wear, I'm part of this world of fashion and money.* And all the shops clamored for attention: *buy, buy, buy now! Keep up, spend, join the party, get with it!* It was all a bit dizzying.

She knew that, for Prune, it must be a kind of ecstasy that came close to torment: wanting everything at once, not knowing what to choose. "But the prices!" Prune moaned. "I just haven't got enough. D'you think Mum and Dad would give me more allowance if I asked?"

"Don't be daft! How can they afford it, when Mum hasn't got a job yet?"

Andie thought that even the wax dummies in the shop windows looked disdainful, haughty as the Rutherfords' cats, their hair glossy and straight, their legs long and smooth, with impossibly thin knees and ankles. If that was how you were supposed to look, Andie thought, looking at her reflection next to Prune's as they gazed in, neither of them matched up very well. She was small for her age, and Prune, though taller, was stocky in build, like Dad, and had wavy brown hair that would never straighten no matter how hard she tried.

Prune let out a sigh of pure longing, and ventured into one of the dim, beat-pulsing interiors, to sort through racks of T-shirts and dresses. Andie stayed on the pavement. She pulled a small sketchbook and a pencil out of her shoulder bag, and began a quick drawing of the models. She liked their poses, their stalky legs, their blank, mask-like faces, their air of being realer-than-real. Not feeling part of all this, and not knowing how to be, she could at least get something to keep, on paper.

She had finished two sketches and started on a third by the time Prune reappeared. "What are you *doing*?" She sounded irritable. "Why didn't you come in? I wanted to show you some jeans I was trying on."

"Did you buy them?"

"No." Prune was downcast. "Only this belt. There

were such groovy clothes in there, And – you should see them! Crushed velvet jeans, tapestry vests, fabulous shoes – but I just can't afford them. How'll I get any decent outfits with just my allowance? I've got to get some money from somewhere, or I'll just die! Everyone else is buying stuff – why can't I?"

"Don't be so stupid! Don't *look*, if it makes you so miserable – they're only *clothes*, for goodness' sake!" Andie stuffed her sketchbook and pencil into her bag. "Can we go now? There must be an art supply store along here somewhere."

"Hey, that looks interesting – across the street." Prune was caught, instantly mesmerized, by a shop called Scene, whose window was squarely occupied by stern-looking models in red and black clothes. "Let's try there."

By the time they returned to Chelsea Walk, Andie felt as if they'd been in every single shop in the King's Road, some of them twice. She'd had quite enough of trailing after Prune, having her opinions ignored or ridiculed. At last, even Prune was tired – despondent as well, having bought nothing but the belt, a purple eyeshadow and a new magazine. As they walked home, she treated Andie to a recital of all the things she desperately wanted but couldn't afford. This time it was Andie who was walking faster and faster, Prune trailing, complaining that she had a blister on her heel.

Back indoors, they both gulped down glasses of juice. Prune went down to collapse in the garden; Andie got out her acrylic paints and her big sketchbook. With Prune safely out of the way, and the apartment to herself, she began to paint.

The vision she'd had in the middle of the night was still in her mind, clear and strong. She began to sketch the outlines, thinking of the colors she would use. A moonscape, eerie and cold. A dark sky. Floating above, as the astronauts would see it, the Earth, smooth and round as a marble, sea-green, streaked with cloud. Tiredness and grumpiness left her, in the concentration of making pencil and paint do what she wanted.

Chapter Four

Through the Roof

"Oh, Andie, you're not painting in *here*!" Mum fussed. "With that dirty water? What if you spill it, or get paint on the sofa? I'd hate the Rutherfords to think we're not taking care of the place. Couldn't you have done that in the garden? Anyway, it's time to put it all away now, and get ready."

Andie had forgotten that they were going down to Patrick's apartment. She tidied up quickly – glad of the excuse, really, as the painting just wasn't turning out the way she saw it in her mind – and changed into a clean T-shirt. To reach the ground-floor apartment, they had to go down their own side stairs, outside into Flood Street, around to the very grand front of Chelsea Walk, and in through the gate. A short flight of steps led up to the door. Dad rang the bell, and the others stood behind him on the steps, feeling self-conscious.

"It's ever so elegant," said Mum, tugging at the front of her blouse. "I wonder how anyone can afford to live here? I'm quite sure *we* can't."

"I know." Dad sounded wistful. "I looked at some real estate listings today – the prices are through the roof."

From here, looking down, Andie could see part of the cellar. There were lights on, and music wafted out through the open window.

"But I thought that was the point?" Prune was saying. "That we're going to find a place of our own?"

Before Mum or Dad could answer, the door was opened by Patrick – the man who'd given them their keys and shown them around when they first arrived. He wore patched, faded jeans and a purple shirt, and his feet were bare.

"Come on in!" He held the door open wide, and they followed him into a spacious hallway with black-and-white checkered marble tiles, and through an archway that led to a wide staircase. "We're all in the kitchen."

Mum was trying not to stare too obviously at everything, but Andie didn't mind gawking. This apartment was very different from the Rutherfords', which was decorated in subdued colors. Here, there were Indian rugs strewn about, and fabric hangings on the wall, beaded and tasseled; the air smelled of joss sticks and spices. Andie was fascinated. In the large kitchen, a woman was stirring something in a pot, and fragrant steam filled the air.

"This is Marilyn," said Patrick.

"Marilyn Foley. Hi," said the woman, who was dressed in a floor-length garment of bright stripes in shades of brown and gold. Her hair was long and mainly loose, some of it pinned up carelessly.

"Pleased to meet you," said Mum, who suddenly looked all wrong in her pleated skirt and slingback shoes. She held out her right arm to shake hands – as if they were at a business meeting! Andie thought – but Marilyn was wiping her hands on a rather stained dish towel, and didn't notice.

"– and you haven't met Kris, have you?" Patrick continued, as a girl in round glasses came into the room. "Kris, this is – er – Dennis and Maureen, that's right, isn't it? – and –"

"Prudence and Andrea," Mum supplied.

"Prue," said Prune.

"Andie," said Andie.

"And I'm Kris with a K. Hi," said Kris, looking at them both with interest. She was quite plump, with a smiley face, and wore jeans and a loose shirt with a vest that could have been made from old curtains.

"Isn't that nice, Andie?" Mum exclaimed. "Someone your own age, living in the same house!"

Andie wanted to shrivel up. Grown-ups ought to know that it hardly ever worked when they said things like that – expecting you to be friends with someone you'd only just met. Besides, it made her feel about eight years old.

"The Kapoors will be down in a minute," Patrick said, fetching glasses. "Amit and Shasha, from the middle floor." He jabbed a finger toward the ceiling. "They've got two children – Ravi, he's twelve, and Sushila who's about sixteen. Both of them incredibly clever."

"Here, try this punch. I can't remember quite what went into it, but it smells good." Marilyn ladled liquid from the pot into glasses, which Patrick handed round; then she poured soda for Kris and Andie. The adults began talking about Wimbledon, and today's win for Ann Jones in the women's final.

"Who cares about boring old tennis?" Kris said to Andie. "I'll show you downstairs, if you want."

"Downstairs?"

"The studio. Where Patrick and Marilyn work."

Studio! That sounded promising. Music studio? Photography? Painting? Following Kris back into the hall, Andie asked, "Do you always call your parents by their first names?"

"Sure, why not?" said Kris. "Patrick's not my father, though. Dad's in America. Patrick's got a son, but he's not around much. It's this way." A wide staircase led up, but Kris went around behind it to a narrow flight that curved down to the cellar.

"Wow!" Andie stopped halfway. It wasn't what she thought of as a cellar, dark and possibly inhabited by rats or mice, but a spacious basement the whole width of the house.

"It's called a half-cellar, really," Kris explained, "because it's only partly below ground level. But that makes it good and light."

The studio was divided into two by open shelving. Each half, one at the back of the house and one at the front, had its own cabinets and workbenches, and was lit by angled spotlights on the ceiling. Gazing around, Andie saw an easel close to one of the windows, canvases stacked against the wall, ink sketches pinned to a cork board, and shelves of paints, and pens, pencils and brushes in jars.

"That's all Patrick's." Kris waved an arm at the easel. "And this side is Marilyn's. She makes jewelry – she's a silversmith. Have you seen that new arcade in the King's Road? East of the Sun, West of the Moon, it's called. She sells her stuff there. It's cool."

"Yes, Prune and I saw it today. We didn't go in, though."

"Prune? Is that really your sister's name?"

"Prue, she prefers, short for Prudence. Prune's my name for her, but she goes crazy if I say it when anyone can hear. So, Patrick's a painter?" Andie was interested in the easel, which had its back to her. "What does he do?"

"He's a graphic designer," Kris explained. "He does all sorts of things – ads, sometimes book illustrations or brochures, one or two covers for record albums. He does mixed media, so sometimes he paints, but just as often it's ink or photographs or collage. Right now he's trying to come up with some ideas for a record company. And he teaches a couple of days a week at Chelsea Art College."

"How fantastic!" Andie could hardly believe that she was living in the same house as a real artist. What could be more inspiring?

Kris shrugged. "It's just a job."

"Yes, but –" To Andie, *just a job* was something you did to earn money. Art was more than that. It was a reason for living.

She moved along the workbench, reverently touching the surface, which was marked with paint and scored by knives. Now she could see the paper attached to the easel with bulldog clips. It was divided into squares, and a pencil drawing was beginning to spread from the top right-hand corner, like a plant reaching out tendrils.

"And you?" she asked Kris. "Do you paint or draw or make jewelry?"

"I fool around with it sometimes. Mostly I'm into drama." Kris was already making her way toward the steps. "I do a lot at school, and go to a youth group. How about you? Do you dig Chelsea?"

"Yes! It's so different from where we live, in Slough. The Slough of Despond, Dad calls it sometimes. It's not really that bad."

Kris smiled. "It's the name – Slough! You might as well call a place Swamp or Slump. What hope has it got?"

Andie rather liked *Slough of Despond*, though. With all the moon talk lately, it made her think of something you might find on the lunar surface, like the Sea of Tranquility or the Ocean of Storms. "Anyway," she continued, "there hasn't been much time to explore yet, around here. I want to go to all the art galleries. The museums. And – well, everything."

"Cool. I don't mind going with you, if you want."

"Really?" Andie had convinced herself that she and her family must seem utterly, hopelessly boring to someone like Kris.

"Sure, why not? I've got loads of time now school's finished, and Sophie – she's my best friend – is in France for the whole summer. We go to Mary Burnet, near Sloane Square. We have to wear straw hats and gingham dresses and knee socks, can you imagine? But it's not bad as schools go, not as prim and proper as you'd think."

Andie giggled, unable to picture Kris in old-fashioned uniform. If Mum and Dad managed to find an affordable flat or house, then of course she'd have to change schools. It might be fun to go to the same school as Kris, even if she had to dress like someone from Enid Blyton's *Malory Towers* stories.

"Your semester ended early," she remarked. "My school doesn't finish till a week from Friday. I'm missing the last two weeks of classes, being here."

"Cool." Kris paused, one hand on the curved banister. "How about tomorrow? You doing anything?"

"Don't think so."

"Good – we'll go out, then. I can't do Sunday – we're visiting someone. Come on. It sounds like the others are here."

The kitchen was now full of bodies and laughter, bright colors and cooking smells. Marilyn introduced Andie to the new arrivals: Mrs. Kapoor, a handsome woman in an embroidered tunic of ruby silk, and her husband, who wore a formal suit and tie like Dad's. The children, Ravi and Sushila, were alike, both rather beautiful. Their hair was black and shiny, and their eyes were the darkest brown imaginable, under smooth brows. Sushila, who was dressed in Indian clothes like her mother, was already talking to Prune by the Aga; Ravi seemed shy, and had retreated into a corner with a handful of potato chips. When introduced, he said hello to Andie with his eyes fixed on the floor.

Soon Marilyn shooed everyone into the living room, which was furnished in rich, dark colors and drapes. She and Patrick brought in food of a kind Andie had never seen before – trays of delicious spicy things, and dips, and little dark-green squarish shapes which Marilyn said were stuffed vine-leaves. Dad heaped his plate; Mum proceeded with caution, nibbling a vine-leaf parcel with great suspicion. Andie tried a bit of everything, liking it all except the olives, which made her think of eyes, and tasted weird.

When everyone had eaten as much as they wanted, there was apple sorbet, served with cinnamon biscuits. Andie and Kris sat together on a big floor-cushion, with Ravi nearby, cross-legged on the floor. Kris took care of the record player, putting on one LP after another. She chose Indian sitar music, and something with a harp, and some jazz – nothing Andie recognized.

After the dishes and plates had been cleared away, Marilyn made coffee and the grown-ups sat chatting. Having dealt with real estate agents and rent, Mum and Dad's list of thrilling conversational subjects had now reached school. "So your two go to St. Dunstan's?" Dad was asking Mrs. Kapoor. "Might that suit Prue and Andrea?"

Patrick passed around a packet of cigarettes, and lit up one for himself and one for Marilyn. Andie's mum, who was supposed to have given up, took one too.

"Come on! Let's go to my halfway place," Kris said to Andie. "The smoke makes my eyes sore."

"What's a halfway place?"

"I'll show you," Kris said, adding, "Coming, Ravi?"

Ravi had been sitting so quietly that Andie had forgotten he was there, but he nodded and stood up.

Kris led the way to the big central flight of stairs. "This staircase used to lead all the way to *your* floor," she told Andie, "before the house was divided up.

Now we've got stairs that lead nowhere – see?" She bounded up to a half-landing, then showed Andie how the next three steps faced a blank wall. This landing had been made into a sitting area, with another Indian rug in jewel colors, and cushions scattered about. "It's my reading place. Reading and thinking. No one bothers me here."

Andie was envious. "You're so lucky! I'm sharing a bedroom with Prune here. At home I've got a room to myself."

"There's always the attic," Kris told her. "Patrick can lend you a key."

"Oh!" Andie remembered the creeping footsteps in the night. "He doesn't work up there, does he?"

"No, he's no need to. He keeps a few boxes of clutter up there, that's all."

"I heard creaky footsteps up there, about midnight. It must have been a ghost," Andie said, half joking, but still wondering.

"No." Ravi was looking at her very seriously.

"There's no such thing as ghosts." It was the first time he had spoken to her.

"But," said Andie, "you can't be sure about that, can you?"

"Well, it wasn't Patrick," Kris told them. "He had an early night, 'cause he'd been out drinking the night before. He was in bed before I was – I heard him snoring. So obviously it *was* a ghost. Our very own ghost. But I've heard it's a friendly one."

She gave a quick, almost furtive glance at Ravi. Andie looked from one to the other; was there something here she wasn't getting? But now Kris was crooning in a spooky voice, holding out both arms with hands dangling. "I am the spirit of Chelsea Walk... *who-oooh!*... I stalk the attic by night..."

"Don't be daft!" Andie giggled, though fear prickled her skin.

"Hey, let's play Murder in the Dark!" said Kris. "We need more people, really, but we can make up special rules for three."

"But it's not really dark yet," Ravi pointed out.

"I know! We'll pretend it is."

They played Murder until it was Ravi's turn to hide, which he did so successfully that Andie and Kris were still searching for him when the adults came into the hallway, and Andie's dad said it was time to go back to their own place.

Darkness *had* fallen by now, and although it wasn't really cold, Andie shivered as she followed her parents in through their side door and up the steep, narrow stairs.

She knew that Kris and Ravi had been hiding something from her, something about the ghost. Maybe it was only a game – or maybe it wasn't.

Chapter Five

Star-struck

"Here," said Mum, handing Andie two half-crowns. "You'll need to get yourself some sandwiches at lunchtime – I expect they sell them in the museum café. Don't be back late, will you? I imagine Kris knows her way around, but phone us if there's a problem."

They were all getting ready to go out. It was Saturday, and Mum and Dad had decided to visit the Tower of London, something they'd meant to do ever since they were married. Andie and Kris were going to the Science Museum, and Prune was spending the day with Sushila. "She seems a very sensible girl," Mum had remarked. "Lovely manners, both those children."

It suited Andie for Prune to have a new friend. Sushila, being sixteen, was probably as obsessed with fashion as Prune was, so they could hang around the King's Road together. Everyone seemed to have enjoyed Friday night: Andie and Prune because they'd each made a friend, Mum and Dad because the neighbors had been so welcoming. Now the Kapoors had offered to have everyone around in a week or two. "But what about when it's our turn?" Mum fretted; Andie didn't know anyone as determined as Mum to turn everything into a problem. "We'll have to invite them all in *here* – and what will I do about food? I'm no good at those exotic things they gave us. A wine-and-cheese party would be more my sort of thing, or perhaps little egg rolls, and sausages."

"Let's not worry about that till the time comes," said Dad, in weekend mood.

Before leaving the apartment, Andie had to submit to the ritual briefing by Mum: "You won't speak to any strangers, will you? Or go off with anyone? Or stay out too long? Or do anything you know you shouldn't? Promise me, now?"

At last she escaped downstairs to meet Kris. Andie's first choice for their day out would have been the Tate Gallery, but Kris seemed intent on going to the Science Museum: "With all the moon stuff going on, they'll have something special there – and besides, it's near Hyde Park. We can go there after."

Oh well; there would be plenty of other days for going to galleries. Andie fell in with Kris's plans, and they caught a bus to South Kensington.

The Natural History Museum, and the Victoria and Albert Museum across the street, looked like vast, ornate palaces, made of stone. The Science Museum, a more modern building, was in the same street. Kris led the way purposefully inside; Andie gazed around, trying to take in everything at once. Where to start? A plan showed that there were three floors of galleries, with signs pointing to Rail Transport, Electric Power, Children's Gallery.

"Space Technology," Kris said, pointing. "We'll save that till last."

It was fun to have the freedom of the whole museum, with no teacher and no question sheet to fill in. They looked at the giant pendulum in the entrance hall, which was supposed to show how the Earth turned on its axis. "Though," Kris said, "we're not going to stand here long enough to see it happening." They passed quickly through Printing, paused for a while at Time Measurement, then went on to Flying Machines, which ranged from the first spidery contraptions to warplanes and models of modern jet aircraft.

Best of all was the space section. There were replicas of the Russian sputniks that had started the Space

Race, and of the Saturn V rocket that would power the astronauts to the moon. Andie gazed and gazed, and thought how strange it would be when it became real – not just something that was talked and dreamed about. The painting she'd finished early that morning – a moonscape – had turned out well after all, in spite of her struggles the day before, with a kind of accidental eeriness that was better than she'd meant. If Kris hadn't been with her, she'd have made quick drawings in her sketchbook now; but seeing Patrick's studio had made her self-conscious. She didn't want Patrick to know that she thought of herself as an artist. But, then again, why not – mightn't he be able to help her? It would be daft to live in the same house as a real artist and never have the nerve to approach him, wouldn't it? Maybe when she knew Kris better...not yet.

They bought sandwiches and sodas at the café; then Kris said it was time to go. "We can come back another day, if you want. It's free, after all." She seemed to be in a hurry, for some reason.

McLean County Unit #5
201-EJHS

Out in the sunshine, they crossed Exhibition Road and a wide, traffic-filled street that bordered Hyde Park, with its avenue of trees. Hundreds of people seemed to be making their way in the same direction.

"Is it always this busy?" Andie asked Kris.

Kris laughed. "No. There's something special happening today. Didn't you know? The Rolling Stones are giving a free concert – and there are other bands too. We can't miss it, not when we're so close!"

"You knew all along? Why didn't you *say*?"

Kris grinned. "You might not have been allowed to come."

Well, no. Andie's mum and dad would never have let her; Kris had guessed rightly. But now that they were here, it would be hard to resist joining the drift, just to see what was going on. They were in a green expanse of parkland, with trees and winding paths, so vast that the buildings on the north and east sides looked very far away. Beyond a boating lake, which Kris said was the Serpentine, the grass was clotted with a mass of people. Most sat or sprawled, some with picnics or drinks; others were dancing to the beat of music that came from a distant stage. Andie and Kris made their way through the crowd, trying to find a good vantage-point, but the figures on the stage still looked as tiny as dolls.

"We should have come earlier," said Kris, disappointed. "We're miles away."

"Is that them? The Rolling Stones?"

"No! The other groups will come on first. We can wait, though – we don't have to hurry back, do we?"

Picking their way, they found a place to sit, a very long way from the stage. Every tree had people gathered beneath its branches, seeking shade. Andie squinted in the strong sunlight, gazing at the scene in front of her. She liked the Rolling Stones – especially, perhaps, because Mum thought them disgraceful – though she preferred the Beatles, especially George.

Kris offered her a mint. "You heard about Brian Jones drowning in his swimming pool? He'd already left the Stones, but all the same I wondered if they'd go ahead and play today. It was only three days ago."

Andie nodded. Last week, while they'd been packing at home, she'd found Prune red-eyed and sniffling in her bedroom, listening to the radio. Prune wasn't, as far as Andie knew, a particular fan of the Stones, but for the next twenty-four hours she behaved as if she'd been Brian Jones's most devoted follower. His photograph now filled the space only recently vacated by Paul McCartney on Prune's bedroom wall. Paul McCartney had been taken down in disgrace, having behaved to Prune with unforgivable treachery by marrying Linda Eastman.

At last, to great excitement from the crowd, the Rolling Stones were announced. Tiny figures came onto the stage; Andie strained her eyes to make them out. She had never before seen a real famous person, and now here was Mick Jagger – it must be him – tiny as a distant fairy, and dressed like one, in a white dress with frills, over white trousers.

"Is that really him?" she whispered to Kris. She had the sense that if she blinked, or didn't believe hard enough, he'd disappear, like Tinkerbell.

"You bet!"

Taking the microphone, the figure who was Mick Jagger said something Andie couldn't hear. The audience fell silent while he read from a book.

"A poem for Brian," Kris whispered. "It's so sad."

Mick Jagger opened a box and released a flutter of white that dispersed into the air. It's like that myth about Pandora's box, Andie thought – except that Pandora released badness. What came out of this box was white butterflies. Wouldn't they be bewildered? Where would they go, in all this space? She knew she ought to be sad for Brian Jones, for drowning, but instead she could only think: there's Mick Jagger. I'm looking at him in *real life*. The dazzle of fame made it hard to believe that a starry person like Mick Jagger walked about in the same world as everyone else, breathed the same air, but there he *was,* on the stage.

The mood had changed. The respectful hush that had settled over the crowd was now an expectant pause. Moments later, the volume was turned up and the drums began to pound a heavy, intoxicating rhythm. People began to sway and cheer and wave their arms to the music as the band launched into songs Andie knew: "Jumpin' Jack Flash", "Midnight Rambler", "Street Fighting Man." The last butterflies flickered and vanished like snowflakes in the sun. A passenger plane flew overhead; a naked toddler stamped his feet on the grass and shrieked with laughter; Mick Jagger's voice rose and fell.

A crowd, while it stayed together, was a living thing, with its own mood, its own ways of behaving. Although Andie didn't know anyone here except Kris, it felt like being in an enormous team, or a club – people who had chosen, just for this afternoon, to link themselves through the hum of expectation, the music and the sunshine, the smell of warm grass and the festival atmosphere. Andie had never felt anything like it before. She thought: I'm listening to the Rolling Stones, in Hyde Park with my new friend Kris. She couldn't make it seem quite real.

When it was all over, and the last whoops and applause had faded, people began to get to their feet, looking surprised – realizing where they were, then gathering their belongings ready to walk across the park and wonder about buses or trains back to normal life.

"I don't feel like going home yet," Kris told Andie. "Let's walk over to the lake. We can get ice cream there."

It was the kind of long summer evening that made for lingering. Kris and Andie walked through the dispersing crowd to the Serpentine, and bought raspberry-ripple cones at the stand there. Then Kris wanted to walk home rather than bothering with a bus, and took Andie on a complicated route avoiding all the main roads, instead taking quiet side streets and alleyways. Sometimes she stopped to show Andie an interesting little shop or recording studio, or an art gallery owned by someone Patrick knew.

"Are you allowed to go wherever you want?" Andie asked, rather envious.

Kris shrugged. "Pretty much. I know my way around, and Marilyn trusts me."

It took an age to reach Chelsea Walk. By the time the back of the houses came into view, Andie was tired and thirsty. And she knew that there would be trouble the minute she got in.

Chapter Six

Grounded

Andie and Kris parted at the side gate, and Andie went
upstairs, hoping that for some reason her parents had
stayed out later than they'd intended. But as soon as
she'd turned her key in the lock, she was met by a hail
of questions.

"Where've you been? What made you so late?"
Mum was hot and flustered. "Why didn't you phone?
You must have known we'd be worried!"

"Andie, you really should have called, if you were going to be as late as this." Dad was less agitated, but still annoyed. "There must have been phones at the Science Museum."

They were all standing in the hallway. Andie pushed past to the kitchen, to fetch a glass of water.

"We didn't spend all day there – only this morning. We've been in Hyde Park. I couldn't phone from there. There was this concert – you know, a free concert, with, er, lots of different groups? And Kris wanted to go, and it was free, and—"

"What – you haven't been *there*? It was on the news. You haven't been to see the *Rolling Stones*?" Mum made the words sound despicable. "Andrea, whatever got into you? You know I'd never have let you!"

"What's wrong with it?" Andie felt herself putting on what Mum called her *young madam* voice. "There were hundreds of other people. Anyone could go – we just sat on the grass and listened. It's this big park."

"I know what Hyde Park is, Andrea. But a pop

concert! The Rolling Stones! Who knows what you might have come across? Drug-taking...LSD or whatever they call it...flower people and all kinds of carrying-on I don't even want to think about –"

"Mu-um! Honestly, *you* could have been there, with Dad – you wouldn't have seen anything wrong – and anyway, there were lots of police—"

"Well, that just proves it!" said Mum in triumph. "The police were there for a reason! On the lookout for drug dealers and pickpockets and the like, I don't doubt. And you two young girls on your own, in the middle of all that! Anything could have happened!"

"But it didn't!" Andie humphed. "We just listened like everyone else, and came home. We're not little kids. Kris is *thirteen* –"

"Yes, and I think it was unwise of me to let you go out with her. We hardly know her, and she's obviously got no idea of what's appropriate. You've hardly begun to find your way around, and that's the first place she takes you! And saying you were going to the Science

Museum? I suppose you planned this yesterday, the two of you? You lied to me?"

"Come on now, Maureen!" Dad tried. "There's no need to accuse Andie of telling lies."

"Anyway, I *didn't* lie! We *did* go to the Science Museum, and I didn't *know* Kris wanted to go to Hyde Park!"

Mum didn't look convinced. "All the same, I'm not happy about this. Not happy at all." She rummaged in the cupboard for plates. "Could you go and call Prue, please? She's in the garden, with Sushila. Tell her I've made sandwiches."

Andie went. From experience, she knew that the best thing was to let Mum calm down, then try to pretend nothing had happened. After all, nothing *had*.

The garden behind the house was bigger than the one at home, and was shared by all three apartments. "It's a bit overgrown, especially at the back," Patrick had said last night, "but I like it that way. And it's great for the kids."

"Kids!" Kris had mocked. "*What* kids?"

It was cool out there now, with dusk not far off. Andie had been surprised to find that there were gardens in London, and she liked this private jungly place far more than the begonias and lobelia Dad planted alongside the front path at home. Nothing here was neat. The high brick walls on three sides were covered in honeysuckle and ivy. Straggly roses breathed out their scent; the grass was rough and uncut, and an area at the back was thick with currant and gooseberry bushes, and an herb bed. Nearer the house stood a tall tree – black walnut, Patrick said it was – with a swing hung by ropes from one of its branches. Kiddish or not, Andie would have tried out the swing to see how high she could fly, if it hadn't already been occupied by Sushila. Sushila wasn't swinging, just idly swaying. Her sandals scuffed the bare earth where other feet had worn away the grass. Prune was sprawled on the ground, a cardigan slung around her shoulders.

"Well, *I* would," Prune was saying, as Andie approached.

"I would what?"

Prune looked round, annoyed at Andie for butting in; Sushila smiled and said hello.

"*What* would you do?" Andie repeated.

Prune sighed; she propped herself up, leaning back on both arms. "Since you ask, we were in the King's Road when someone came up to us. Well, up to Sushila. She was from a...a model agency. Andromeda, it's called. She wants Sushila to go and have some photos taken." She gave Andie a tight smile.

"Oh!" Andie swiveled around to look at Sushila. "And will you?"

"Course not. It's probably just a trick," Sushila said. "They'd take the photos and charge me a fortune for them, and that's the last I'd ever hear."

"You could at least *call* them." Prune's voice was thick with envy. "Just to ask."

"But I don't want to be a model," Sushila told her, swinging gently. "I want to be a doctor."

Prune didn't answer, but plucked a stem of grass and chomped on it.

Andie guessed how it had been: this model agency person homing straight in on Sushila, ignoring poor old Prune. Sushila looked gorgeous enough, just as she was, with messy hair and no makeup, to be on the front cover of *Honey* – you just couldn't help looking at her flawless milky-coffee skin, her dark eyes and the way her smile lit up her face. Isn't that just typical, Andie thought, the way things get dished out? Sushila was not only beautiful, not only brainy enough to want to be a doctor, but – it seemed – nice as well, not at all conceited. Prune was just, well, ordinary. No matter how hard she tried with hair straighteners and foundation and mascara, she'd never look as good as Sushila, even when Sushila did nothing at all. Maybe Prune thought she'd be infected by Sushila's glamor if she hung around with her.

"Did you have a good time, Andie?" Sushila asked.

"Er, yes. Kris and I went to see the Stones in the park."

"Oh! So did we."

Andie looked at her, then at Prune. "*You* went?" She wondered whether Prune would get an earful from Mum, too, when she went in.

"Couldn't miss something like that, could we? Wasn't it fab? Wasn't it just out of this world? And so *sad*, the poem for Brian, the butterflies..." Prune gave a tearful smile.

"Don't start, again," Sushila said, nudging her with one foot. It was like they were already best friends. So Prune had cried in the park – well, Prune would, Andie thought. She could see it now, the kind of crying that's actually quite enjoyable – *look at me, I'm crying.*

Sushila got up from the swing and stretched, then reached for a fringed bag that lay in the grass. "Let's go in now. I'm hungry."

"And Mum's making our tea," Andie remembered to tell Prune.

A small cream card, with *Andromeda* embossed on it in black, lay on the grass where Sushila's bag had been. Andie saw Prune reach out for it. But she didn't give it back to Sushila, or say, "Here, you dropped this." Instead, with a warning look at Andie, she hid it in the palm of her hand, and slid it into her own bag.

Chapter Seven

Ascent

Andie might have guessed. As punishment for going to the Stones concert, she wasn't to be allowed out with Kris for the next few days. "And then," Mum stipulated, after tea, "only if you tell us where you're going, and come back at the time we agree and not a moment later."

"So it's all right for Prune," Andie grumbled, "but I do exactly the same thing and get punished for it?"

"Andie, Prue's sixteen," said Mum. "So's Sushila. I can't say I'm delighted about them going, either – but there's a big difference between twelve and sixteen."

"But you're being so *unreasonable*!" Andie clattered the cat dishes into the sink. "What's the point of being in London if I'm not allowed to go anywhere? I might as well go back home and stay with Nan, if I'm going to be kept prisoner here."

"Now *you're* being unreasonable," Mum told her. "Exaggerating ridiculously. No one's locking you in prison. If the agency doesn't come up with work for me tomorrow, I'll take you to Selfridge's. You need new shoes for school."

"Don't want to go to Selfridge's," Andie grumped. "'Specially not to buy stuff for *school*! Not before summer's even started!"

"I know it hasn't. And we're going to enjoy being here," Mum said firmly.

"*Enjoy!* When I'm not allowed out? I bet Marilyn

and Patrick aren't making all this fuss, just for Kris wandering over to Hyde Park!"

"No, I don't suppose they are. But they're – well, much more free and easy than we're used to." Mum made a tight, prim face. "I don't think they're even *married*. He's Patrick Sharp, but her name's Foley, I think she said. All this permissive carry-on we keep hearing about! They're *living together*." She made it sound like a criminal offense. "Not the sort of people we usually mix with."

"You can say that again. They're about five hundred times more interesting."

Mum stood squarely, hands on hips. "Now you're being rude, on top of everything else. I think it's high time you were in bed, young lady. And try to get out on the right side, in the morning."

𝕮𝕭

Andie must have slept for a while – Prune had come in and got ready for bed without disturbing her – but she'd been fully awake for at least half an hour, her mind full of the day's sights and sounds, excitements and arguments.

And now her eyes were wide open, and her ears straining for a sound from the stairs.

She was sure she'd heard something, a creak, like someone trying not to be heard. Yes – there it was, creeping on up, toward the attic.

A tremor ran down Andie's spine – excitement, as much as fear. It could be Patrick, going up to fetch something from one of his boxes, or to put something up there. But why would he do that so late at night, when the whole house was asleep? Only if he had something to hide. What if he was an art thief? Andie's thoughts raced. She imagined Patrick sneaking paintings – small ones, miniatures would be easiest – out of the National Gallery, tucking them inside the front of his jacket. Then he'd store them in the attic until the next dark night, when his accomplice would bring a riverboat to the nearby pier on the Thames, and smuggle them out to sea, to Holland or France...

Or what if it wasn't Patrick at all, but a madwoman who lived in the attic? Patrick's real wife, perhaps – the reason he wasn't married to Marilyn! Andie's class had read *Jane Eyre* this year, and her favorite bits had been about Mr. Rochester's mad wife who roamed the corridors at night and clawed at people with her nails and set fire to bed curtains with the candles she carried. That would be even more exciting than stolen paintings. But if this was the Madwoman of Chelsea, she must be going *back* to the attic, not leaving it...

There was only one way to find out. Before Andie knew she'd decided what to do, her feet swung out of bed onto the rug and nudged themselves into her sandals. A dim light from the street lamp, filtering through curtains, was enough to show her the bedroom door, and out to the hallway. The door to Mum and Dad's bedroom stood open; she heard Dad's snuffles as he turned over.

She mustn't lock herself out! Looking round for something to hold the door ajar, she found a sort of wooden rack with umbrellas in it. She managed to lift it into place without making a loud *thunk,* and slipped past it to the tiny, windowless landing outside.

Compared to the grand staircase that swept up from the ground floor to Kris's halfway place, these stairs were plain and narrow, with a handrail fixed to the wall. After the top-floor landing, where she stood, another flight led to the attic rooms. Looking up, Andie felt the down-draft of dry, dusty air, and shivered. No light was showing. Who – or what – could be creaking round the attic in darkness? And *why*?

For a second she considered going back in, getting back into bed and forgetting she'd heard anything. Perhaps she hadn't. Maybe the sounds were only those of an old house settling into itself, creaking under its own weight, settling for sleep. But then she heard, unmistakably, the sound of footsteps above her head.

Slowly, gripping the handrail, she mounted the stairs. On each one she paused, fumbling for the next with a raised foot. Her eyes and ears were boring into the dark, her heart thumping so strongly that she felt it would throw her off balance. At the turn of the stair she stopped and glanced back at the wedged-open door. If a spectral figure appeared ahead, or if someone flew out at her – a madwoman with nails like daggers – she could scuttle back down and in, and lock the door behind her.

Creak – creak. She couldn't stop the pressure of her feet from making a faint sound, seeming to echo in her ears and up into the roof space.

But what if it were faster than she – the thing up there? It might rush down the stairs and into the apartment ahead of her...shut her out...

Now the creaks were answered by the quick light steps of someone above. Someone moving towards her. She froze, unable after all to run back; fear clamped her feet to the stair, her hand to the rail.

A dark figure appeared in the attic doorway, and stopped there.

"Who's that?" it said, in a quite ordinary voice: certainly not the way she'd expect a madwoman or a vengeful ghost to sound.

"It's me," Andie told it. "Andie."

The figure seemed to nod. "Shh!" it went, and beckoned her to come on up.

More curious than frightened, Andie followed. A flashlight flicked on, and the dark space sprang into brightness. She was standing, with this other person, on a narrow landing, up in the very top of the house, beneath the slope of the roof. The flashlight beam turned to her face, harsh and dazzling.

"You gave me a fright," said the voice.

Chapter Eight

Skyhopping

"Who's that?" Andie said, blinking.

"Me." The person holding the flashlight swung it back to show his own face. She saw glossy dark hair, brown eyes, white smiling teeth. It was only a boy, and a little shorter than her. Ravi! Ravi Kapoor, from the middle apartment.

"What are you *doing* up here?" She was sagging with relief.

"Skywatching," said Ravi. "Or I will be, in a minute."

"But it's dark!"

"I know! That's the whole point! Wouldn't see much in the daytime, would I?" Ravi shone his flashlight at the bare floorboards, illuminating a telescope and folded tripod, a notepad, and a book called *The Sky at Night*.

Andie was puzzled. There were no windows here, no way out that she could see. "Why from here? Why don't you look out of your own window?"

"Because there's a better view from the roof."

"The roof? You climb the roof in the dark?"

"Haven't you looked up at it, from outside? I don't perch right on top, like an owl. There's this flat bit."

He was picking up his equipment – slinging the tripod over one shoulder by its strap, picking up the telescope with loving care. He nodded toward the book and notepad. "Bring those, if you're coming. You want to come and see, don't you?" he added, a touch impatiently, when she hesitated. He seemed so different from the painfully shy boy he'd been at the party.

"Sure," said Andie. It began to seem like an adventure.

Treading softly, Ravi led the way past two open doors that led into rooms stacked with cardboard boxes and crates. "Those used to be maids' bedrooms. No one uses them now. There's this bigger space behind for storing stuff, as well. If it were my house, I'd turn it into an observatory."

Andie was tiptoeing behind. "Are you allowed up here?"

"Well, sort of. I used to come up with Dad. But now I come on my own."

"Is it yours, the telescope?"

"It is now. Here's where we go through." Ravi reached into his pocket for a key, and unlocked a low door in the side of the storeroom. "My uncle gave it to me when he got a better one – he does a lot of birdwatching in India. But this one's quite good. It's a refractor. I got it in January – Dad and I used to come up in the evenings, then. But there's not enough darkness this time of year, so I wake myself up in the night."

Andie followed him through the door, surprised to see a narrow walkway, edged by a low wall. Peering over, she found herself at the front of the house – and saw, a long way down, the garden railings, the gate, and the row of trees that separated Chelsea Walk from the Embankment. It was brighter here than in the attic, because of the street lamps, the lights strung across the Albert Bridge, and the illuminated buildings on the south bank of the Thames.

"Don't look over if it makes you dizzy," said Ravi. "I'm not good with heights."

Andie looked for a few moments longer, to show him that *she* wasn't scared – even though the sight of the long drop made her stomach clench tight.

"It's fantastic!" She turned to face him. "It reminds me of *Mary Poppins* – have you seen it? That song about the rooftops of London?"

"The chimney-sweep's song?" Ravi was moving along the walkway, his flashlight beam shining ahead. "Come on. I usually go around the back. You can't get away from street lights in London, but it's a bit better around the other side."

Andie saw that the walkway led all the way around the top of the house – through a sort of valley between this roof and the one of the next-door house – to the back, where she now looked over the highest branches of the swing tree and over other gardens and roofs and chimneys. There was a steady, low hum of traffic.

Ravi was setting up his tripod, bracing its legs, screwing the telescope to its mount. "There was a bit of cloud earlier, but it's clear now."

Andie had been too busy looking down, and noticing where she was putting her feet, to glance up. Now she did, and the dazzle of stars seemed to fly at her. *Look! Look at us! Why don't you spend every night gazing in wonder? What could be more mysterious, more magnificent than we are?* There were more and more stars as she gazed, as if they were pushing through blackness from as far as her eyes could see. And farther on than that, there would be stars and stars and more stars, and dizzying dark that must go on forever. When Andie's brain tried to stretch far enough to take in the idea of *forever*, it balked and jammed, refusing to believe something so impossible. But that only led to another impossibility: if forever reached an end, what was beyond that?

"Come on," said Ravi. "We'll go skyhopping. It'll be good tonight. Ever done it before?"

Andie stared. "Are you mad?" But what if he really *is?* she thought. What if he thinks we can balance on the wall and stretch out our arms and fly, like Superman to the planet Krypton? Or is he planning to call up some obedient little spacecraft to take us from one twinkling star to another, light years away?

Ravi didn't look mad. He was adjusting the height of the telescope, swiveling it on its mount, adjusting the eyepiece.

"Skyhopping means getting a fix on a constellation you're sure of, then setting off from there to find others," he explained. "You know the Big Dipper? How to find the Pole Star?"

"I think so," Andie said, not *quite* certain.

"Well, there it is. See?" He pointed. "You don't even need binoculars to find that. See the Big Dipper shape, and Polaris, the very bright one? I've got the scope lined up on that. Have a look. You need to get it right for your own eyesight, so turn this dial till it comes clear."

Andie looked. The stars sprang out at her in fresh brilliance.

"It's part of Ursa Major," Ravi was saying, "the Great Bear. See –" He had opened his book, and now shone the flashlight on a page which showed the constellation in diagram form – though Andie couldn't see much resemblance to a bear. "That's how the first astronomers found their way around the sky. Made their sky-maps. They saw the shapes of birds and swans and bears. And that must be as long ago as there have been people on Earth."

"Where's the moon?" said Andie. "I want to look at the moon."

"We'll have to go around the side."

Andie followed Ravi back into the valley-between-roofs. She was trembling with excitement as he swiveled the telescope and adjusted it. She was about to see the moon as she'd never seen it before.

"There." He stood aside; she moved over to look.

The moon seemed to thrust itself toward her, pale and enormous. She saw its strange, pitted surface so well that she imagined herself standing on it, with powdery moondust at her feet. It had mountains, whole ridges of them, and huge flat plains; it was a *place*.

"Do you think the astronauts will really be able to land there?" she asked Ravi, still peering into the eyepiece.

"Oh, I expect they'll land all right," Ravi said, matter-of-factly. "It's whether they can take off again that I'd be worried about."

Andie looked at him. "Doesn't anyone know?"

"Well, it's never been tried before, has it? They can't be *certain*."

"They must be so brave!" Andie felt a thrill of excitement and fear. "Just imagine, being stranded – looking at the Earth, knowing you can never get back – would you do it, if you had the chance?"

"Like a shot! Wouldn't you?"

Andie thought. "Yes. Yes, I would," she said, after a moment. It felt strange to say this, because in her mind she'd been there already – walked about on the moon's surface, and gazed back at the Earth. But she wasn't going to tell Ravi, because it would sound stupid. In silence, she studied the lunar surface again. She gazed and gazed until she began to shiver, aware for the first time that she was only in her pajamas. Ravi was dressed more warmly in jeans and a sweater.

"I can't believe how close it looks," she said. "As if we could hop over to it and walk about."

"I know. It's nearly a quarter of a million miles away, but that *is* close, compared to anything else we can see. The next nearest thing's Venus, and that's twenty-six million miles, but only at its closest."

"How do you know so much?" she asked him.

"I just read books, and I look at the sky, and notice things and look them up."

"What about sleeping? Don't you sleep?"

"Of course – but I'll stay a bit longer. I want to see – hey!"

He broke off as Andie barged into him, startled by a pressure against her legs, a warm furriness.

"The cats!" she exclaimed. "I forgot – I left the door open!"

Panic jolted through her; she felt trembly and stupid. How could she have been so careless?

"What, those big soft kitties?" Ravi flashed his flashlight around, revealing a back view of

Rumpelteazer, ginger striped tail held high as he stalked along beside the parapet.

"Rumpelteazer!" Andie whisper-called. "Come here – puss, puss! Oh no, I bet they're both out – Mungojerrie! Rumpelteazer!"

"They're not easy names to call out..." Ravi was moving slowly along the walkway on the other side of the door.

Andie's mind was racing. They could go anywhere – escape over the roofs and chimneys of the whole row of Chelsea Walk... She pictured them perched on the highest chimney stack, yowling at the moon like cartoon cats. What if they don't come back? What if they fall? What if –

Slinking after Rumpelteazer, she wondered whether to grab him – but would he skitter away, even scale the roof? Luckily, he seemed less sure of himself out here than he was indoors. He hesitated, looked at her over his shoulder, turned and meowed. She darted forward.

"Gotcha!" She tightened her fingers round his collar, and picked up his heavy, resistant bulk. Carrying him back in triumph, she saw that Ravi had gone inside, to the storeroom. Rumpelteazer's weight made her arms sag as she ducked through the low door. The glow from Ravi's flashlight swept round the room, illuminating beams, cobwebs and more boxes and bundles.

"*Yesss!*" went Ravi, as the light picked out black Mungojerrie stalking a spider in a corner. "Shut the door –"

Andie struggled to do so, her arms full of protesting cat. At least, now, Mungojerrie couldn't go gallivanting over the rooftops. Ravi was stalking him, holding out one hand as if offering a morsel of food. The cat hesitated, his eyes reflecting greenly. Ravi pounced; Mungojerrie yowled and hissed, but he was caught.

Giggling with relief, Andie followed Ravi down the stairs, treading carefully. At the open door of the flat, she moved the umbrella rack aside and went in;

Ravi shoved Mungojerrie through after her. She held the door open just a crack, enough to speak, not wide enough for the cats to slip out again. "Thanks!" she whispered. "I'd better stay in now. But I liked the skyhopping. Can I come next time?"

"Sure. I'll tell you when."

"I won't tell anyone if you don't," she added; but he was already ghost-footing up the attic stairs again, heading back to his telescope and the countless millions of stars.

Chapter Nine

Crash-landing

"You know what, And – you're *good*."

Andie looked up from her sketchpad, astonished. It was unusual for Prune to say anything complimentary. But, yes, Andie was pleased with the drawings she'd done of the stilt-legged models in the King's Road shops, with their perfect, haughty faces and their strutty poses.

Prune turned her head on one side for a better look,

adding, "They need better clothes, though. The ones you've given them are just ordinary."

"I don't really do clothes." Andie had just sketched in vague short dresses, or flared trousers.

She was sitting on the garden swing, Prune looking over her shoulder. Evening sunshine filtered through the branches of the walnut tree; pigeons cooed, and a thrush was singing somewhere nearby. It wasn't late, but Andie was tired, after the excitement of the night, and a full day. Mum and Dad, relenting a little, had taken her to the Tate Gallery; they'd spent the whole morning there, then had a sandwich lunch on the Embankment and walked all the way home. Andie's mind was afloat with paintings and sculptures, color and shape – Turner and Blake, Rousseau and Rossetti, and more recent work that was made entirely of dots or wavy lines or bits of metal. Mum and Dad had tisked at those, and moved briskly on to the Turners and Constables, but Andie had wanted to see everything. Now her head was filled with so many images that she hadn't known what to draw first. She had come out to the garden in the hope of seeing either Kris or Ravi, but neither of them seemed to be about. Flicking through her sketchbook, she had found the drawings from Friday, and had just been doodling. But the doodles had turned themselves into a whole series, and her pencil had worked away at them while her mind was elsewhere.

"Could I have some?" Prune asked.

"Have some what?"

"Some of your drawings. You could do them with –" Prune giggled – "with no clothes on. I mean just do the outlines in soft pencil, and I'll add the clothes. I like designing. I've got loads of ideas, but you know how hopeless I am at drawing."

"Well, okay." Andie shrugged, turned a page and started again. If it kept Prune in a good mood, it was worth doing. And it might give her a bargaining tool for later.

ᬒ

Mum's secretarial agency had found her a temp job for the week, shorthand-typing. She was up early to get breakfast for herself and Dad, dressed in her cream suit, and fretting because she said her hair was a mess, although to Andie it looked exactly the same as usual.

"If you go out, you must go together," she told the girls. She was wiping down the drain board, which was already spotless. "Andie, remember what we said about not going out with Kris. And don't be late back. I'll be preparing dinner for half past six and I want you both in long before then."

Andie agreed reluctantly, wondering if she could persuade Prune to catch a bus to the National Gallery. But Prune had other ideas. As soon as Mum and Dad had left, she retreated to the bedroom, where she spent nearly an hour getting ready to go out.

"I'm meeting someone," was all she would say.

"Who?"

"No one you know."

"Can I come?"

"No!"

"Well, that's great! Mum says I can only go out with you, and you don't want me!"

Prune didn't answer, gazing at herself in the mirror, mascara wand in hand. Andie wondered if she'd met a boy; she was certainly going to a lot of trouble with makeup, so it must be someone she wanted to impress. It couldn't be Sushila she was going out with; Sushila and Ravi's school, St. Dunstan's, didn't finish till Friday.

"So what am I supposed to do?" Andie persisted. "Sit indoors all day, on my own? That'll be fun!"

"You can do your painting, can't you? Down in the garden? Then it won't be like staying in. When I get back, we'll go for a walk or something."

"Big deal!" Andie humphed.

When Prune finally left, after examining herself from all angles in the mirror and changing her top three times, Andie went downstairs to see if Kris was in. She was, and suggested doing what she called a "Bridge Walk": crossing the Thames on the nearest bridge, back on the next, and so on. "We can easily get as far as Westminster Bridge, then we can go in St. James's Park as well. I once did it all the way to the Tower, but it's a bit hot to walk so far."

Andie agreed immediately. She didn't want to tell Kris about the prohibition; it made her feel like a little kid. Anyway, it was quite obviously Prune's fault: *she* was the one not doing what Mum had said. If Andie got in before Mum did, and preferably before Prune as well, no one need know.

It felt seasidey by the river, standing on the Embankment looking down at a passing tourist boat whose wake made ripples that fanned out to the shore. There was even a faint smell of saltwater. Busy traffic crossed the bridge, but along the promenade people were lingering, taking photographs, eating ice cream. Andie liked the mixture of holiday and busy Monday.

"Did you come on your own?" she asked Kris. They were on Westminster Bridge, watching the pleasure boats and the drabber, more workmanlike barges that passed underneath. "That time you walked all the way to the Tower of London?"

"No – that was with Ravi. It was his idea, actually – bridgehopping, he calls it. He's awfully quiet when there are people around, but fun when you get to know him."

What a strange boy he was, Andie thought – bridgehopping, skyhopping! She opened her mouth to tell Kris about her nighttime adventure on the roof, but closed it again and said nothing.

☙

As soon as she let herself into the apartment, she heard Prune crying. Really crying – face down on her bed, sobbing hard.

"Prune! What's wrong?" Andie rushed in, fearing a dreadful accident to Mum or Dad, at the very least.

"Nothing!" Prune turned her face into the pillow, her shoulders heaving.

Andie sat on the bed beside her. "Don't be daft!

What is it? Were you attacked or something? Has something awful happened? Come on, *tell* me!"

Prune continued to sob and gulp for a few moments, then sat up angrily and grabbed at a tissue from the box on her bedside table. "They were horrible, that's what! So horrible!"

"*Who?*"

"The people. The snooty people at the agency."

"Agency? What, Mum's temp agency?"

Prune glared at her. "Don't be dense! You know! The people at Andromeda – the model agency. Sushila wouldn't go, so I went instead – called and made an appointment and they said they'd see me. But they – they –" She started to weep again, tears spilling. Her eyes were already panda-like, smudged with black mascara that made sooty trickles down her cheeks. "They hardly even looked at me! The girl at reception – the way she sneered, you'd think I was something that had crawled in under the door. Then she sent for this other woman, the one who spoke to Sushila in the

King's Road. She looks like Marianne Faithfull, only much older – up close you can see her eyes are all wrinkly. She didn't even recognize me! It was only Sushila she was interested in. Just looked me up and down, then said where was my portfolio – photos, she meant. And of course I haven't got any. But then she said – she said –"

"Come on! *What* did she say?"

Prune could hardly get the words out between sobs. "She said – I haven't – haven't – haven't got the looks or the bone structure – or the figure – I'm too *big* – I – I – I could make myself look a lot better but I'm just – just not model material – oh, Andie! You should have seen the way she looked at me, all snooty – like I'm substandard or something, a reject –" She grabbed another tissue and blew her nose hard. "And she went, 'That friend of yours, with those gorgeous exotic looks, we could do something with her. But you're not what we're looking for, I'm afraid, darling.' *Darling!* She really called me darling, only it sounded like an insult. And the reception girl sort of snickered – she didn't think I heard it, but I did – so I just turned around and walked out."

"Well, I'm glad you walked out," Andie said with feeling. "They sound awful! Why'd you want to have anything to do with people like that? As for saying those things – of course you're not substandard! Snobby cow. Don't take any notice."

"But how *can* I not take notice? You don't understand, Andie, you just don't get it – I want to be a model more than anything else, and if I can't do it, I don't know what the point of anything is – and Sushila could do it if she wanted, only she doesn't, and it's such a waste – oh, you don't know how *useless* it makes me feel!"

"Don't be daft! Of course you're not useless. Are you going to let that bossy woman tell you what to think of yourself, just 'cause you're not an identikit Chelsea Girl?"

The answer was obviously *yes* – Prune dissolved

into another tearburst. Andie looked at her in dismay. To be quite honest, Prune looked terrible – her eyes red and puffy, her makeup streaked, her mouth stretched sideways with crying. Andie had been about to say, "That was only one agency. You could try others." But that would surely lead to more disappointments. Prune was never going to turn herself into one of those sleek girls with their racehorse legs and pouty faces and straight glossy hair, the girls she saw every time she opened a magazine or went to the King's Road. Instead, Andie said, "You look nicest when you're just you. When you're not trying to look like everyone else."

"But I *want* to look like everyone else!" Prune wailed.

Andie felt rebuffed. She was doing her best, but nothing she said could make Prune feel any better. She tried to care as much as Prune did, to see how it felt. She thought: it'd be like someone telling me I'll never be any good as an artist, no matter how hard

I try. It'd feel like one of my arms or legs was useless, and might as well be chopped off.

"Come on! You'd better stop crying before Mum and Dad get in," she told Prune. "You don't want them to know where you've been, do you?"

"No," Prune said, in a muffled voice. She got up from the bed, and went through to the bathroom.

ᖉ

Later, in bed, Andie listened for telltale creakings from above, hoping that Ravi might be skyhopping again. Not a sound. Disappointed, she wondered whether to creep out of the apartment and go up to the attic, just in case the door was unlocked and Ravi was up there. But while she was still dithering, she fell asleep.

Chapter Ten

Mountains on the Moon

Kris was away for part of the next week, visiting a cousin. With time to herself, Andie painted and painted. She worked at the kitchen table, so that Mum wouldn't fuss about spilled water and stained carpets. Pleased with her moonscape, she made a whole series – fantastical landscapes with rocks and ravines, craters and crevices. She used harsh, bright colors that made the settings look larger than life.

At night, when she looked out of the window at the real moon, it felt like sharing a secret with it. But what sort of secret could it be, when the TV news and the papers were full of the approaching Apollo 11 launch? There were charts, diagrams, interviews, discussions – and it was still more than a week away.

And what about Ravi? When would she have the chance to look at the moon properly again through his telescope, or to stand lost in wonder at the huge spread of blackness and stars? She saw him only once – out in the garden with his mother, who was snipping mint from the herb bed beyond the shrubbery. Ravi had just come from school, and wore a brown blazer and a brown and white striped tie.

"Hello there, Andie! Isn't it a lovely day?" called Mrs. Kapoor, and Andie went over hoping to talk to Ravi. Maybe Mrs. Kapoor would go indoors with the mint; then Andie could ask Ravi when he was next going star-watching. But he only said hello, in an awkward, formal way, then made an excuse and went indoors, and it was Mrs. Kapoor who stayed.

"You'll have to excuse Ravi. He's so shy, especially with girls," she told Andie. "I hope you don't think he's unfriendly. He doesn't mean to be."

But Ravi *hadn't* been unfriendly, or even the slightest bit shy, when they'd been up on the roof! He'd been a different person – confident, fun. Andie was mystified. Had she upset him, somehow? Or only dreamed about being outside with him in the middle of the night?

Prune remained doleful and downcast, though she tried to hide it when Mum or Dad were at home. She lay out in the garden on a towel, trying to get a tan, and complaining that the high walls and the walnut tree gave too much shade; all the same, she managed to get herself sunburned and sore. Without telling Mum, who wouldn't have approved, she had bought herself a bikini – bright pink, with turquoise stripes – but was too self-conscious to let anyone but Andie see her in it. If anyone came into the garden, she made a grab for her towel, and shrouded herself from shoulders to ankles.

Andie did the sketches Prune had asked for, and Prune tried to draw clothes on the models, getting cross and frustrated when the drawings didn't turn out as she wished. "*You* do it, Andie!" She flung down her latest attempts on the kitchen table. "I just can't get them right! I'll tell you what I want, and you can draw it."

Anything for a quiet life, Andie thought. She put her own painting carefully to dry, and drew and drew to Prune's instructions. The results, they both thought, looked good. Andie had expected Prune to want frills and beads and floaty dresses, but the designs were surprisingly tomboyish and practical. Fashions For The Future, Prune called them. Since the clothes could be worn by either boys or girls, Andie developed a face and hairstyle to match – longish sleek hair, and a handsome face that could be either male or female.

On Wednesday, Maria, who was Mrs. Rutherford's cleaner and came once a week, interrupted Andie and Prune in the kitchen. "Hey!" she said, bending to examine the drawings. "Ought to work for a fashion magazine, you two! I could see myself in that jumpsuit, if I lost a pound or two. Very Space Age."

"There, you see," Andie told Prune later. "Even if that stupid agency didn't want you as a model, that's not the only way of working in fashion. You could be a designer."

"Thanks, And. I owe you a favor." Prune collected up the sheets, and put them into a special folder, which she referred to as her portfolio.

Andie was quick to cash in this favor, before Prune forgot or changed her mind. Next day, she asked Prune to go with her to the National Gallery. Prune managed it with barely a complaint, though she got bored fairly soon and sat reading about "How to be a Switched-on Dolly Bird" in her magazine. "Dolly bird!" Andie scoffed. "Haven't you had enough of that? Who wants to be a *doll*? Something to dress up in pretty clothes, and that's all?" But it wasn't worth starting a real argument, not when she was having her own way. They bought sandwiches in the café, then Prune left Andie for an hour and a half while she went to investigate the shops in the nearby Strand. "Nothing like the King's Road," was her verdict. "More like Mum's sort of shops." But Andie had seen Renoir and Pissarro and Monet, and was happy.

That evening Prune went down to see Sushila. Andie was reading in bed when she came back, bringing with her a book called *The New Astronomer*. "Ravi said to give you this. What's going on?"

"Oh, nothing!" With great curiosity, Andie took the book and opened it. "It's...to help with my painting, that's all."

Tucked inside the flyleaf was a small, handwritten note. "*ROOF – TONIGHT – MIDNIGHT*" it said, in capital letters.

She could so easily have missed it! Or been asleep,

and not even opened the book till tomorrow! Now, tingling with excitement, she prepared to stay awake for the next two-and-a-half hours. She turned the pages, looking at diagrams of the constellations. Maybe, if she concentrated, she could impress Ravi by recognizing some obscure star pattern, or by mentioning that Galileo Galilei, who'd lived near the Leaning Tower of Pisa, had made a telescope good enough to see the mountains of the moon. In 1610! And it was Galileo who thought the moon had seas, though it didn't really, and had named the Sea of Tranquility, where the astronauts would be landing. Of course Ravi would know all that – this was his book – but maybe she could work it casually into the conversation.

Prune got ready for bed, but sat fiddling with her transistor radio; Mum and Dad were still up, watching *Wojeck,* Dad's favorite crime drama. Andie kept an anxious eye on the time. Her parents were usually in bed by eleven, but what if they stayed up late? How would she escape then? At one point, in spite of her worry, she almost dozed off – but then snapped her eyelids open and pushed herself up from the pillow. She dreaded being fast asleep in bed, while Ravi waited for her on the roof. Not that he *would* be waiting, with the night sky for company – Cygnus the Swan, and Sagittarius the archer, and Ursa Major and Minor, which meant Great and Little Bear. It was hard to make herself believe that what looked like scatterings of bright dust was actually made up of distant suns, fixed in their sky patterns. She flicked back to a colored picture of the solar system. The diagram made it look as if some observer had stood right outside the Earth, noting distances and orbits and colors. But, she thought, it's been worked out by people standing just like I did, staring up at the sky – looking and comparing and puzzling – and asking themselves questions about how it could possibly make sense. People used to think the sun went around the Earth, didn't they? – she'd just read that

Galileo had even gone to prison, for saying it was the other way around.

How astonishing it was! How had she not been fascinated ever since she was old enough to gaze up at the sky?

She heard footsteps in the hallway. Mum, in her dressing gown, looked in the door.

"Put your light out now, Andie. It's time you were asleep. Goodnight, love."

It was ten past eleven. Prune was already sleeping. Andie clicked off her bedside lamp and waited until her parents were in their room and the apartment was dark, allowed a little longer for them to fall asleep, then turned her light back on and continued reading.

At last! Five to midnight, and all quiet. While she was putting on socks and sneakers, and pulling a warm sweater over her pajama top, she heard the faint creak that meant Ravi was on his way up to the attic. She tiptoed out of the apartment, remembering to leave the door only slightly ajar this time, so that the cats couldn't escape.

He was there, setting up his tripod on the flat part of the roof. Andie gazed up. The night was beautifully clear, the sky dense with stars – luring her closer, making her wish she could spread her arms and fly into them.

"Hello! It's lovely and clear tonight. I want to look at Lyra," Ravi said, just as if he hadn't virtually ignored her in the garden, last time they'd met. "It's only small but it's got one of the brightest stars in it, Vega."

"Does Kris know you come out here?" Andie asked, while he was adjusting the telescope.

"Of course! That's why she was winding you up about the ghost. She knew it was me," Ravi said, with his shy grin.

"Wouldn't she want to come, too? I mean, Patrick and Marilyn let her do whatever she wants – she wouldn't have to sneak out, like I do."

"She did come up a couple of times. But she's no

good at staying awake, or waking up once she's gone to sleep – and when she did, she had to stay in bed till ten in the morning, to get over it."

"It's just – you know," Andie tried, "I don't want to leave her out."

Ravi looked at her in surprise. "Leave her out? Who's leaving her out? She's not interested, and we are, that's all. But I was telling you about Vega. You can't miss it, even with just your eyes – it's the fifth brightest star of all. Fifty times brighter than our sun. That's a useful one for skyhopping. Here, look through the scope. See it, the really bright one?"

"Yes, I think so."

"And if you look really closely at Delta," Ravi continued, "which is left and a little bit down, you'll see that it's really a double! Can you see the two separate stars, very close together?"

"Yes!" Andie said, after searching for a few moments. "And they're different colors – one's sort of reddish, and the other one's white."

"That's right. Now look with just your eyes, and I'll show you the Summer Triangle – a triangle made by Vega and two other bright stars, Deneb and Altair. That's useful to know, as well...gives you a good, er, landmark..."

"Skymark?"

"Okay then, skymark."

Soon Andie had various skymarks she could pick out for herself – even if she'd never know as many stars by name as Ravi did.

"But they're moving!" she exclaimed, finding that she had to keep making slight turns of the telescope.

"They're not. *We* are. The Earth's turning – the stars stay where they are."

"Well, of course." Andie tried to pretend she'd always known this. And of course she *had* known – but how odd to see it happening, almost to feel it!

"Now let's come a lot closer to home," Ravi said, when Andie was quite dazzled. "To the moon, I mean."

He positioned the tripod and focused, muttering,

sounding pleased, then motioned Andie toward the eyepiece. As before, the moon's surface leaped toward her, startling in its detail. It wasn't just a decoration in the sky, a flat silver disk like a floating coin, or smooth like a Christmas-tree decoration. It was real, huge, *there* – the telescope brought its surface features sharply into view, mountain ridges, craters, peaks, valleys, cracks. Some parts looked as dimpled as orange peel, some were craggy with cliffs or smooth as lakes. Andie had just seen in the book that all the mountains and craters and plains had names; there were detailed maps. Some astronomers, it seemed, knew the moon better than Andie knew the back garden at home.

"I feel dizzy." She stepped back from the telescope at last. "Moon-dazzled."

"That's the best kind of dazzled," Ravi said, taking over. "Next to sky-dazed, or star-giddy."

Andie looked up. It was true – the stars did make her giddy, as her eyes reached farther into their depths, and more and more of them seemed to rain at her, pouring through the immensity. She stretched out her hands and saw stars shining between her spread fingers: worlds and worlds contained in the span of a hand. I'm starbathing, she thought. Better than sunbathing – that only makes you hot and red. Starbathing fills you with time and space and wonder.

 C3

She tried to do it in paint – to show the blackness of space, pricked by points of light as far as the eye could see, and the mystery of *forever*. But paint just wouldn't do it. It was only a spotty mess. Every time she thought she was getting better at painting – every time she did something she felt proud of – her next attempt would show her how much she just couldn't do. Her eyes saw, and her mind saw, but in between them and the paper were her clumsy hands.

Sometimes she felt like giving up. But only sometimes.

Chapter Eleven

East of the Sun,
West of the Moon

Prune's birthday was coming soon. As Prune had such definite ideas about what she liked and didn't like, Andie thought it would be safest to let her choose her own present. This meant a shopping trip, to look for something Andie could afford – a record, perhaps, or a rope of beads or some bangles. Andie braced herself for a morning of watching Prune drool over things she couldn't have, and off they went to the King's Road.

The present was found and bought with surprising ease – a Simon and Garfunkel album, which cost more than Andie had had in mind, but was very definitely what Prune wanted. But, of course, Prune hadn't finished yet.

"I want to look in East of the Sun, West of the Moon." She grabbed Andie's arm; not waiting for an answer, she pulled and shoved her through stationary traffic to the shop entrance on the other side of the road.

A lanky young man, with straggly hair and a beard that made Andie think of paintings of Jesus, stood by the open door, smoking and gazing out into the street. His thoughts seemed to be elsewhere; he gave the girls a vague nod as they passed. Prune marched straight in; Andie followed, feeling like someone entering a different, intriguing world, like Narnia. East of the Sun, West of the Moon wasn't just one shop, but a sort of indoor market, made up of separate stalls, some with their own entrance doors or bead curtains. Inside was shadowy and enticing, smelling headily of joss sticks and patchouli and cotton, lit with tiny lamps strung around the ceiling and from the partitions. Andie saw rugs in earthy colors, kaftans, belts and beads, mirrored cushions, Indian bowls; sitar music lured her farther in. A few customers were browsing, but no sales staff were in evidence.

"Marilyn's jewelry's in here," Andie reminded Prune. "You know, Kris's mum."

Jewelry of various kinds was mounted on a stand at the very back of the arcade. Andie and Prune gazed at rings, necklaces, beads, bangles, chokers and earrings, displayed against a backdrop of midnight-blue velvet. Marilyn's pieces, pinned to a board headed *Foleyworks,* were of finely-wrought silver in the shapes of fish, snakes, moons and twining patterns, some studded with tiny gemstones of turquoise or black. Also on the stand were heavier pieces by other designers – made from bronze, gold or wood, decorated with shells, feathers and many-colored beads.

"Oh! I love this – I just love it!" Prune lifted a carved ivory bracelet and slipped her hand through it, turning her wrist this way and that. "I saw one just like this in *Honey*, with a safari jacket and skirt. Doesn't it look great?"

"How much?"

Prune flipped over the small handwritten price-tag. "Fifteen pounds! But it *is* real ivory."

"No one in their right mind would spend that much on a *bracelet*," Andie said. "Anyway, it's dead elephant. You wouldn't wear dead elephant, would you?"

"No-o." Prune sounded doubtful, but took off the bracelet and replaced it on the stand.

They wandered on, Prune to a rack of tie-dye T-shirts, Andie to a stall draped with silky Indian scarves. Prune took ages, dismissing half the clothes, examining others with minute detail, then finally choosing a tiger's-eye ring from the jewelry stall.

"Come on!" Andie was impatient. "I'm hungry. Let's go home and get some lunch." She looked around for someone to take Prune's money. There seemed to be only the Jesus-man, who was still standing by the door smoking as if he had nothing else to do. She wasn't even sure that he worked here; but as they approached, he moved to a cash register on the nearby counter.

"Just this, please." Prune took a ten-shilling note out of her purse to pay for the ring.

The man gave her half-a-crown change, then looked at her searchingly and said, "Just by the way, what about the bangle?"

Prune's cheeks flushed red. "What bangle?"

"The one in your bag. Are you thinking of paying for that as well?"

"I don't know what you mean," Prune stammered.

Andie looked at her, aghast. She knew Prune well

enough to recognize guilt when she saw it. The young man really did look quite a lot like Jesus, or at least how Andie imagined Jesus to look. He had sad hazel eyes that rested reproachfully on Prune's face, and thin cheeks as if he didn't get enough to eat. He was even wearing a thin and slightly dirty white kaftan that looked a bit Biblical.

"Hey," he said. "I saw you slip that bangle into your bag when you thought no one was looking. I'm not going to get heavy about it. It's no big deal to me. It's only money when it comes down to it, and there's more important things to worry about. It's your conscience, not mine. Who's to say a thing belongs to one person rather than another, just 'cause he's paid money for it? If you want it that badly, take it – go on. I'm just telling you that I *know*."

Andie was fascinated. Prune, turning ever-brighter scarlet, looked incapable of saying anything at all, so Andie chimed in, "Actually, if that bangle belongs to anyone, it's the elephant whose tusks it's made out of.

I don't see why people should cut off bits of animal to make jewelry, when there are other things they could just as easily use."

The Jesus-man looked at her with interest. "Well, you've got a point there. I can dig that. See, I don't eat animals, or wear animals, or use anything from animals. But hey, who said it was an ivory bangle? I didn't."

"Well, I –" Now it was Andie's turn to feel her face firing up. He must think *she* was involved in this. "Why are you selling ivory, then, if you don't want to use animal stuff? That doesn't make much sense!"

"It's not my shop," he said pleasantly. "I'm just standing in for a friend who's gone traveling."

Andie couldn't quite see where the conversation had got to, or how it might end. This young man wasn't actually asking Prune to empty out her bag, or threatening to call the police. And Prune wasn't marching out of the shop in a temper, or trying to make a run for it – but she wasn't denying having the bangle, either, which would surely be her response if she *hadn't* got it.

"Come on, Prune!" Andie said, impatient to be gone. "Have you got it, or haven't you?"

"Prune, was that?" The Jesus-man was leaning on the counter with both elbows. He had a very nice smile, Andie noticed.

"Prudence. Prue. Anything but Prune," Prune said, flustered. She reached into her crochet bag, and, shamefaced, drew out the carved bangle and handed it over. "I'm sorry – I must have—"

"Zak? What's going on?" called a female voice. There was a jangle of bead curtains behind the register, and a wild-haired woman with an Indian scarf tied as a headband came through to join the Jesus-man. Unlike him, she had a very businesslike manner, and piercing blue eyes that seemed to take in the situation at one glance.

"Oh, nothing. We were just chatting," he said.

He covered the bangle with his hand, and pushed it under a folded scarf near the till.

Andie gave him a *thank you* look, said goodbye and hurried Prune out to the sidewalk.

"What's got *into* you?" she hissed. A girl burdened with shopping bags tisked as she veered round them into the road. "Prune? Were you really going to *steal* that?"

"I don't know! I – I – no, of course not! I must have put it in my bag by mistake."

"Really?" Andie peered at her closely. "Well, you were lucky that Zak guy was so un-heavy about it. You could have been arrested! Prune, you can't go around helping yourself to stuff!"

"I don't!"

"Not much, you don't. It's like that Biba dress in the wardrobe. You see something and you've just got to have it. Honestly, you shouldn't be allowed out!"

"It was a mistake!" Prune flared back. "Don't you ever make a mistake?"

"Not mistakes that make me steal from shops, no!"

They'd started to walk in the direction of the Town Hall, but now Prune stopped, taking hold of Andie's sleeve. "Andie – you won't tell Mum, will you? Or Dad?"

"No," said Andie, "as long as you promise not to do it again. By mistake or on purpose. I don't want a jailbird for a sister, thanks."

"He was nice, though, that Zak, wasn't he? Weird, but nice."

"Yeah," Andie retorted, "and I bet he thought you were really great. Trying to lift stuff, then standing there red as a beet. A gibbering beet."

"I didn't gibber!"

"Yes, you did. It's a good job I was there, or you'd have melted into a bright red gibbering jelly."

Very huffy with each other, they walked home in silence.

Chapter Twelve

Everyone's Gone to
the Moon

By Sunday, the ban on going out with Kris had
expired. Kris came up to see if Andie wanted to go to
Hyde Park again – not for a rock concert this time, but
to wander around the Serpentine and eat ice cream,
and look at the outdoor art exhibition.

"The what?"

"All these artists come out on Sundays and hang

their paintings on the park railings. Some of it's terrible – well, most of it really, but there's some good stuff as well. And there are people who do portraits while you wait, or cartoons. That's fun to see."

Mum had to agree that Andie could go, but went through a list of *dos* and *don'ts*, ending with: "*Don't* be back later than six. I mean that, Andie."

"What's with your mum?" Kris asked, as they waited for the bus. "Why's she so strict?"

"Oh, she's just not used to...well, to London. She likes it, but she thinks I'll get lost or kidnapped the second I leave the apartment." Andie felt an uncharacteristic desire to stand up for her mother. "They're a bit disappointed today, Mum and Dad. They went to look at some apartments yesterday, but they turned out to be much too small." And dilapidated, Mum had said, and none too clean, and not on streets she'd want to live on, either. "That's one drawback to staying here in Chelsea Walk," Dad had pointed out. "We're getting used to standards of luxury we'll never afford for ourselves."

"Oh, too bad," Kris sympathized. "I hope you find somewhere fairly close, anyway."

Andie could have told her that there was little chance of that. Real estate agents' details were arriving by post several times a week, but, as Mum put it, what she could afford she didn't like, and what she liked she couldn't afford. To make it worse, there was an apartment for sale farther along Chelsea Walk, but when Mum had rung to ask the price she had put the phone down again very quickly.

Andie wasn't going to let today be spoiled. She and Kris did some very splashy rowing on the Serpentine, then walked all the way across the park to Speaker's Corner, where, Kris said, anyone could stand up on a box and make a speech. "Only no one's doing it today. Quite often someone's on about the love of God or macrobiotic diets or miners' unions, or whatever they're into. Votes for women, it used to be – did you know a suffragette used to live in your apartment? Even went to prison, Patrick told me. She was

Anne Rutherford's great-aunt or something."

But now here were the paintings, the artists, ranged along the outside of the park fence, so that Bayswater Road had become a linear art gallery. Pictures were hung from the fence or propped against it – landscapes, portraits, fantasy scenes, prints, pastels, oils or delicate watercolors, enamel work, miniatures, models and sculptures, sewn pictures and collages – every kind of artwork Andie could imagine. Most had price labels on them, and were much less expensive than Andie had seen in shops. She looked at the people with interest, because they were artists like her. Some were sitting on the ground, one was even asleep, curled up with her dog on a big cushion, while others tried to chat with passers-by or offered to draw them as caricatures.

Kris had very definite tastes, marching past anything she didn't like, straight to those pictures that caught her eye. The ones she liked best looked Chinese, in bold ink and wash, and somehow gave the effect of sweeping rain.

"If I could paint, that's the sort of thing I'd do," Kris said. "Only there are chimpanzees who can paint better than me. How 'bout you?"

Andie hesitated, then said, "I do paint. Painting's what I do."

Kris looked at her in surprise. "Why didn't you say? I mean, I'm no artist, but I'd like to see your stuff."

"I don't know." Andie wished she'd kept quiet. "I mean – you live with Patrick, a rea– I mean, he's a professional. What I do would seem like fooling around."

"But that's how everyone starts. Trying things. Seeing what works and what doesn't. He does a lot of fooling around himself. You will let me have a look, won't you? Oh, go on! I'd really like to."

"Well, perhaps," Andie said cautiously. Maybe Kris would forget about it, or was only taking a polite interest. But when they got back to Chelsea Walk, and Andie was about to say, "Bye, see you tomorrow," Kris said, "Wait up – what about your paintings? Aren't you going to show me?"

"Well, all right. But only if you don't say anything to Patrick. Promise?"

"Why?"

"I don't like people seeing them. I mean, *you* can – but anyone else, it's kind of too risky. We've got this awful art teacher at school who thinks I'm rubbish, and – if anyone else tells me that, I might start to believe it."

Kris shrugged. "Okay. I promise not to tell you you're rubbish."

"But then," Andie said, newly anxious, "you mustn't say you like them unless you really do!"

"Andie – just get them, will you?"

They went upstairs. Mum was getting tea in the kitchen; Kris chatted to her, in her easy way, while Andie went into the bedroom and took her paintings out of their folder. She hadn't shown these to anyone else: not Prune, not Mum, not Dad. Mum would only say, "Very nice, love," or something as empty as that; Dad might advise her to paint baked-bean cans instead and call it Pop Art.

Andie laid out the paintings on Anne Rutherford's candlewick bedspread, and fetched Kris.

Kris looked at them without speaking, while Andie remembered how critical she'd been of the paintings in the park – giggling, derisive (though not within earshot of the artists), pouring scorn on those she dismissed. I shouldn't have given in, Andie thought. They're mine – private. When someone else looked at them, it was as if the paintings were pinned in the glare of harsh spotlights that showed up all their flaws. She frowned, knowing they weren't good enough. What was it, with her own work? No matter how pleased she was when she'd finished painting, or when she looked at her work last thing at night, it took less than a day to become dull and flat, no better than anyone else could do. Now her moonscapes looked garish and clumsy, the colors too bold, the perspectives all wrong.

"Andie!" Kris finally said, and her voice was full of reproach.

☙

"TARGET MOON" was on the front cover of the *Radio Times*, with a picture of a rocket lifting off. Moon excitement was everywhere; the papers and the TV news were counting down the days to the Apollo 11 launch on Wednesday. The astronauts, Buzz Aldrin, Neil Armstrong and Michael Collins, had to practice being weightless, and moving around in their bulky suits that made them look like space toys. It would take till Sunday for them to reach the moon. How amazing, Andie thought, to be going where no human being had ever been before! Would it change them for ever? How could you fly to the moon, then come back home to ordinary life?

They would collect samples of moon rocks and moondust and bring them back to be analyzed. From that, scientists hoped to learn more about how the moon had formed – whether its mountains were really volcanoes, how its craters had been made, whether there was or had ever been water on the moon, and how far it was similar to Earth. The likelihood of the mission succeeding was discussed endlessly. Even if the astronauts landed on the moon, what were the chances of them returning? What if the lunar module simply sank into the moondust and disappeared? Or what if the astronauts *did* come back, but brought deadly bacteria with them?

"Everyone's Gone to the Moon" was being played again and again on the radio. Andie heard the words, over and over in her head, while she worked on her paintings. Although she knew it was silly, she didn't like the thought of *everyone* watching the moon, thinking about it, wondering; it made it less *hers*. The moon would surely prefer to be left alone.

In her pictures, though, she could roam the moon of her imagination.

"Hey," Kris had said, in the bedroom. "You're *good*, Andie! Really good!"

Andie felt herself glowing all over again, remembering. Kris wouldn't say that just to be polite. Andie was encouraged, and continued painting. Her moonscapes became ever more intricate, their colors more intense. The Earth, reduced to a coin-sized disk in the sky, floated above, casting cool greenish earth-light, reflected from the sun.

Mr. and Mrs. Kapoor invited everyone in the house to a Moon Party that weekend, which would start late on Sunday night and go on through the early hours of the morning. It seemed likely that TV coverage would continue all night long, so that the moon landing could be shown as it was happening. Andie's head reeled at the idea of TV coming live from the moon – like watching *Dr Who* or *Star Trek*, only this would be real, actually happening, while people all over the world gazed at their television screens.

The semester had finished now at St. Dunstan's, and Sushila was busy helping her mother with fundraising for the Indian charity she worked for. Prune spent her afternoons in the Kapoors' apartment, putting leaflets into envelopes, addressing them and taking bundles to the post office. At least,

Andie thought, Prune wasn't likely to get into trouble while she was with sensible Sushila.

Ravi seemed to spend quite a bit of time playing cricket, or practicing with friends, but sometimes Andie saw him in the garden, or coming in through the side gate. Once he was playing chess with Kris under the walnut tree: "But it's so *boring*," Kris said. "He always wins."

While Andie watched, Ravi finished off the game in three decisive moves. "Checkmate *again*!" Kris moaned. "And just when I had something really clever worked out."

Ravi gave one of his shy looks from under his bangs. "But you'd complain if I let you win."

"Well, of course," Kris humphed. "If I win, I want to win properly. Some chance."

Ravi was already putting the chess pieces away in their box. Although Andie had only the most basic idea of chess, she would have liked a go, if he'd asked; but he only said, "See you later," and went indoors.

"I don't get it," Andie said to Kris. "Sometimes he's friendly, and sometimes he isn't."

Kris smiled. "No, it's not that. He likes to keep his friends in separate compartments. Me for chess, a friend from school for cricket practice, someone else for swimming."

"And, er, me for star-watching, then," Andie confessed. "While you were away, and once before."

Kris didn't seem particularly surprised. "Prowling round the chimneys at night? Moon mania, that's what it is. There's no getting away from it. Even I'm starting to get hooked."

 C3

There was more skywatching on Tuesday night. At last, with practice and the help of *The New Astronomer*, Andie was finding more of the skymarks for herself: not just the Big Dipper but the whole of Ursa Major, and Casseiopia, and Lyra and the Summer Triangle. The night sky was changing from a confusing sprinkle of stardust into recognizable constellations and clusters.

Soon, though, hazy clouds put an end to gazing, and Ravi unscrewed the telescope from its tripod.

It was Kris's idea that the three of them should go to the Science Museum on Wednesday, to watch the Apollo 11 launch live from America. Ravi must have decided that this was a special enough occasion for him to be with two friends at once, and agreed.

Lots of people had the same idea. Opposite the elevator on the second floor, a room was set aside for radio broadcasting, and a demonstration of color television, which Kris and Andie had seen on their first visit. Soon, people who could afford it would have color TV in their own homes, just like going to the movies. But for the moon mission, a much larger screen had been installed, with a direct link to Cape Kennedy. Andie, Kris and Ravi joined the crowd of people – adults and children – who had gathered in the warm, stuffy room, some standing, some sitting on the floor.

The launch tower made Andie think of the Eiffel Tower in Paris. Next to it, tethered and steaming quietly, was the Saturn rocket, elongated and elegant, like something from *Thunderbirds*. The astronauts were already on board, right at the very top, waiting. The television showed them eating their breakfast earlier, steak and eggs and orange juice, looking like people getting ready for an ordinary day at work; then, bulky and padded in their spacesuits, being driven to the launch pad, going up by elevator to the command module, and being helped inside.

It would be a while yet. Andie felt too tense to watch any more. What must it be like, belting yourself into the top of a space rocket, knowing that some people estimated their chance of returning as only fifty-fifty? She wandered off with Kris into the adjoining gallery; Ravi wouldn't budge, but stood absorbing every detail.

Excitement mounted as time for the launch drew near, with more and more people packed into the room, those outside getting as close as they could to the doorway. Andie lost Kris altogether in the crush, and could just see Ravi toward the front of the audience. Nothing seemed to be happening, nothing at all, but "Four minutes and counting," said an American voice, unbelievably calm. A countdown began on the screen, stretching out the seconds for longer than felt possible. "Ignition sequence starts – six – five – four – three – two – one – zero –" Andie held her breath, and everyone around her seemed to be doing the same; there was the tiniest of pauses before the rocket began to lift. Andie had expected it to soar off at extreme speed, like an exploding firework, and was astonished that it could rise so slowly – more like an elevator going up, she thought, than the great whoosh she'd expected. "All engines running – tower cleared—" and the commentator's voice was drowned by clapping and cheers and exclamations. The rocket was soaring now, with a fiery tail; just a slim, pencil shape.

Everyone's gone to the moon. In their imaginations, anyway. It was hard to think about much else.

Chapter Thirteen

Down to Earth

"Don't go out after supper, girls," Mum said, with her head in the larder. "We need to sit down and talk."

Andie was feeding the cats, Prune helping to put the shopping away. Andie glanced at Prune for a reaction, but got only a shrug in reply. *Sit down and talk?* Last time that happened, it was to tell the girls about the move to Chelsea. Now? Was it about *staying* in London? Had Mum and Dad found their dream apartment or their perfect house? But Mum didn't sound joyful or excited. It was more the tone of voice she'd used after reading Andie's school report – disappointed, resigned.

They had to wait till Dad was home, and they'd eaten cold ham and salad, and canned peaches with cream. Then, when everything was washed and put away, and the kitchen wiped and scoured to Mum's satisfaction, and coffee made, they all sat round the dining table.

"I'm sorry, girls, but this is going to be a big letdown," Dad began. "Things aren't working out quite as we hoped."

They'd obviously planned this. Dad sounded as if he'd prepared a speech; Mum sat gazing sadly at the tablecloth.

"Your mum and I have been to lots of real estate agents and read all the property pages," Dad went on, "and been to see some apartments, as you know. There's no way around it. We've had to realize that we just can't afford the sort of place we'd like. Either we'd have to settle for some tiny apartment, far too small for the four of us – or live so far out that we may as well stay put, in Slough."

"What?" Prune burst out. "You mean we're just going back home?"

"But what about your job?" Andie asked her father. "That was the whole reason for coming here, wasn't it? You're not going back to your old one?"

"No, no." Dad shook his head. "I'll stay with the new job. *That's* going well, at any rate. I'll just have to commute from Slough every day."

Prune looked disgusted. "But I don't want to go back to boring old Slough! I like it here!"

"I know, love – we all do," said Mum. "But we've got to be practical. We can never afford an apartment like this. We'll just have to enjoy staying here, while it lasts. We've got another two weeks."

"It means there's no need to change schools," Dad added, "and you've both got your friends back at home—"

"I've got friends *here,* now! So's Andie. I want to stay. It's not fair, bringing us here and letting us get used to it, then dragging us back to that dismal dump of a house."

Mum straightened. "Dismal dump? That's our home you're talking about, Prue. Dad and I worked hard to get it. It wasn't easy. We used to *dream* of having a home of our own—"

Prune sighed. "Don't let's start on ancient history!"

"Shut up, Prune!" Andie kicked her under the table; Prune gave a yelp, and glared back. "What's the use of whining?"

Mum sighed. "I did think we could have a sensible *discussion.*"

"What's the point?" snapped Prune. "You've made your minds up, haven't you?"

Dad shook his head. "It's more a question of having our minds made up for us."

So, Andie thought, everything will be back as it was. She'd be back in the navy uniform of Hillsden

High, waiting at the bus stop for Barbara each morning. It would be nice to talk and giggle with Barb again, and sit at the back in Math where they could pass notes to each other, and take their packed lunches out to the bench by the sports field when it was sunny – but what about Kris and Ravi? They were her new friends. She wanted to see Barbara, but she wanted Ravi and Kris as well, that was the problem.

"You're quiet, Andie," said Dad. "What are you thinking?"

"I – I was thinking about school. I quite liked the idea of going to the same school as Kris."

"But, Andie," Mum said gently. "Mary Burnet is a private school. We could never afford for you to go there. It would have been St. Dunstan's for you and Prue."

Andie hadn't even thought of that. Everything around her had slumped into dullness – but still, she couldn't see the point of going into a Prune-like sulk. It wasn't Mum and Dad's fault. If they couldn't afford to live in London, they couldn't afford it, and that was that. She glanced around the dining room – at the table that was polished by Maria once a week, at the glass cabinet full of crystal glasses, at the elegant chairs they were sitting on. We just don't belong in a place like this, she thought. We've only been kidding ourselves, pretending.

"Tell you what," Mum said brightly, "why don't we plan a nice day out for tomorrow? The four of us?"

"Good idea." Dad was trying to sound cheery. "There are lots of tourist things we've not done yet. How about Madame Tussaud's?"

"I don't want a nice day out." Prune sat hunched and defiant. "And I'm definitely not trudging round staring at a lot of stupid waxworks. What's the point?"

Only two days ago, Prune had told Andie that she *wanted* to go to Madame Tussaud's. In this mood, she wasn't likely to be pleased with anything.

"Come on, Prue," Mum tried. "You're not being fair. It's not just a whim, you know, this change of plan –

Dad and I are disappointed too. We really thought we could live in London. But it's just not possible."

"It's not *my* choice, commuting," said Dad. "Setting my alarm for the crack of dawn – waiting for trains – getting home late and tired. But let's be positive. I've still got the job."

"It's not good enough, though," Prune huffed. "It's always money, isn't it? Why's there never enough?"

"Prue! Let's keep a sense of perspective, shall we?" said Dad. "We won't be begging on the streets! We're lucky, when you think about it – *more* than lucky. I'm bringing in a reasonable salary with this new job, your mum's got the skills to find work anywhere, we've got a roof over our heads and a home of our own, and we've got each other. Let's be grateful for all we *have* got, instead of pining for what we can't have."

"Have you finished the lecture?" Prune was getting to her feet. "I'm going to see Sushila."

How was it, Andie wondered, that the moon was a short rocket-hop away, but the move from Slough to London was too far to be managed? She went down to find Kris, and tell her the news.

"Oh, that's too bad," Kris sympathized. "But surely there's some way around it?"

Andie couldn't think of one. She didn't understand money – how, for people like Patrick and Marilyn and the Kapoors, it didn't seem to be an issue. They just had plenty of it – enough not to be always talking about it, anyway.

"I've never not lived in a city," Kris said. "London or New York. Can't imagine anything else."

Patrick was downstairs in the basement, working; classical guitar music floated up the steps. I've been living in the same house as an artist, Andie thought, and I've hardly spoken to him. What was he working on? In a brighter mood, she might have asked if they could go down and see – then, maybe, she might mention, or Kris might mention, her own ambitions...

"I want to be an artist – I really, really want it, more than anything in the world," she could say, "but my parents don't think I can. What should I do about it?" Whenever she'd imagined this, she'd decided that it could wait till later – till she felt more confident, or had more pictures to show. But now there wouldn't be much later; it was all coming to an end, and soon.

She felt weighed down with gloom. Her dream seemed as unreachable as the most distant stars. In just a few weeks' time, she'd be back in Miss Temple's dreary class, in that dull room where even the air seemed gray and tired. Back to the scrubby brushes, the spongy paper and the colors drained of life.

Chapter Fourteen

One Giant Leap

Andie had never stayed up so late – it was past three o'clock in the morning! – and was now watching the TV screen through a haze of tiredness. They were all in the Kapoors' apartment, clustered round the television in chairs and on floor cushions. Everyone was there – Marilyn and Patrick, Kris, all the Millers and all the Kapoors.

The lunar module had landed, and now everyone

was waiting – "the world waits," as the TV commentary kept saying – for the astronauts to emerge, and the first pictures.

"Do you realize," said Mr. Kapoor – he'd asked them to call him Amit, though Andie couldn't quite bring herself to; he was such a quiet, dignified person and seemed to know so much – "that never before have so many people watched the same event at the same time, all around the world?"

"But only those with access to television and electricity," said his wife. "Hundreds of thousands of people haven't got these things, and to those people – if they hear of it at all – this must seem completely irrelevant. But I have to admit, it's very exciting."

"We'll remember this, for the rest of our lives," Dad said solemnly. "It's history in the making."

Ravi, of course, had gone into the shyest of silences, hiding inside himself, the way he did. No one would guess that he had more than a passing interest in what was happening. Why did he have to be so secretive? Andie wondered. But, when she considered it, lots of people had secrets – *she* did. Perhaps everyone needed a secret self, one that was more real and true than the outside everyday self, that other people saw.

"I bet this'll be commonplace by the time you kids are as old as I am," Patrick remarked. "This is the Space Age. There'll be regular sightseeing trips to the moon. Space cruises."

"Holidays on Mars," said Kris. "Vacations on Venus. Count me in!"

"The Russians won't want to be outdone," Dad said. "I bet they'll have men on the moon before long."

"Or women," Sushila added. "One of the first Russian cosmonauts was a woman – Valentina someone."

"Tereshkova," Ravi put in.

"Valentina Tereshkova. That's right."

Kris said, "Who's going to be the first woman on the moon? Why should men have all the fun?"

"I don't agree with all this women's lib stuff," said Mum. "Women wanting to be just the same as the men. Where's it all going to lead?"

Did she *have* to come out with such squirm-making remarks? "Mu-um!" Andie reprimanded, out of the corner of her mouth.

"You'd better not say that too loudly in the upstairs flat," Patrick said, smiling at Mum. "The ghost of Edwina Rutherford might come back to haunt you."

"Edwina Rutherford?"

"Jeremy Rutherford's aunt. It used to be her apartment – she left it to him when she died. She was a suffragette – went to prison for it, more than once – very formidable lady, she must have been—"

"Shh! Something's happening –"

Everyone watched the screen, listening, waiting. Andie thought of all the attention focused on these men – Neil Armstrong and Buzz Aldrin, the two who were in the Eagle, and actually on the moon's surface, while Michael Collins stayed in the command module. Poor him! To go all that way, and not make the final descent to the moon! It must be like not being picked for the hockey team, only thousands of times worse. But what if it all went wrong, and he had to return to Earth alone? What if the other two, down on the Moon's surface, couldn't take off again, couldn't get back to the command module? What if the first men on the moon were also the first to *die* there? They must be so brave, accepting the huge risks. Like the crew of Apollo 1, who had all died when their rocket exploded on the launch pad...

Snatches of fuzzy conversation could be heard, or sometimes not quite heard, between the module and mission control at Cape Kennedy. Crackly voices – sounding far away, though certainly not a quarter of a million miles away – exchanged remarks and sometimes even jokes. It was Neil Armstrong whose voice had said calmly, "The Eagle has landed," from what was now called Tranquility Base, and who came slowly, blurrily into focus, as *FIRST LIVE PICTURES*

FROM MOON came up on the screen. On leaving the capsule, he had lowered a TV camera, which was now – amazingly – sending back images! At first, Andie couldn't tell what she was seeing; it looked like a snowy landscape with some sort of building in the foreground. Then she realized that it was a ladder, and a part of the spidery module, and that the large pale shape moving slowly down was Neil Armstrong himself, stepping carefully just like Dad had done when he wallpapered the lounge. "I'm at the foot of the ladder," he said, speaking to them live from the moon – from the moon itself! "The surface appears to be very, very fine grained as you get close to it – it's almost a powder." He hesitated on the lowest step. "I'm going to step off the ladder." A bigger drop, some fuzzing and blurring, and his voice again: "That's one small step for man, a giant leap for mankind."

Everyone was talking at once. "That's it! Man on the moon!"

"Wow! Unbelievable!"

"They've done it! They're there!"

"The moon's a real *place*! He's standing on it –"

"How must that feel? To stand where no human being has stood before, ever?"

"Amazing! Incredible!"

"*A* man, he must have meant to say," said Sushila. "One small step for *a* man, a giant leap for mankind. Doesn't make sense, otherwise."

They all watched while Neil Armstrong collected samples of moondust and moon rocks. A few minutes later, Buzz Aldrin came carefully down the ladder, guided by Armstrong – bobbing like an inflated toy in the moon's reduced gravity. And now the two were talking to each other: "Isn't that something? Isn't it fine?" It sounded so ordinary; they might have been on the beach at Brighton. Andie had expected them to say something more startling, something wise and wonderful. But what? Perhaps "Wow!" and "Unbelievable!" and "Isn't that something?" were the best that could be done with words, when you saw something utterly astonishing. Perhaps a person standing on the moon wouldn't quite be able to believe what he'd seen and done, till much later. Perhaps not ever.

Neil Armstrong aimed his camera at what he called "the panorama," the view from where he stood – the surface of the moon, pale, flat, pockmarked. But it wasn't Andie's moon. She had the odd feeling that *her* moon was somehow more real. Part of her longed to go back there, by herself.

The two astronauts put up an American flag and posed beside it.

"That doesn't seem right," Sushila said. "It's like they're claiming the moon for America."

"The plaque says *for all mankind*," Kris pointed out.

"I know, so it ought to be an Earth flag. Or no flag at all."

"An Earth flag! Now, that would be something," agreed Sushila's mother. "I can't help thinking that all those billions of dollars this has cost would've been better spent on reducing poverty in Africa and India. It seems dreadful that people starve in Biafra while these colossal sums are spent on landing two men on the moon."

"Shh, shh, here's Richard Nixon."

Now the President of the United States was speaking to the astronauts by telephone from the White House. "This certainly has to be the most historic phone call ever made," he said. "For every American, this has to be the proudest thing of our lives, and for people all over the world." It sounded like he was reading a speech. "Because of what you have done, the heavens have become a part of man's world."

"But they always have been," said Ravi. "People have always looked at the stars, and tried to make sense of them."

He immediately looked embarrassed at having said so much. A few moments later, when his mother went into the kitchen to bring in cakes and sweet pastries and coffee, he followed her out of the room, and didn't come back. Andie guessed that he'd escaped to the attic. She was torn between staying to watch the television, and following him outside to look at the real moon.

It was Kris who noticed next. "Where's Ravi? I can't believe he's missing this!"

"Gone to bed?" Patrick said, yawning. "It'll be hardly worth it if we stay up much longer."

"If I know Ravi," said Mr. Kapoor, "he'll have gone up to the roof. He's got a telescope now – his uncle gave it to him."

"On the roof?" Mum looked puzzled. "How does he get up to the roof?"

Andie tried not to turn red.

"There's a way out through the attic storeroom. It's quite safe," Mr. Kapoor told her. "You've been up there, I expect, Kris?"

"Sure," Kris answered, then, to Andie, "How about now? I don't think I'm going to bed at all. Coming?"

Andie followed her very quickly, before anyone could think of a reason why not.

It was already far too light for stargazing. Toward the east, along the river, the sky was pale mauvey-pink, streaked with faint clouds. The low moon was faint, silvery, two-thirds of it in shadow; present even when it appeared to dissolve into daylight. Although it was ridiculous to imagine she'd see the American flag staking its claim across a quarter of a million miles of sky, she felt reassured that the moon looked as pale and untroubled as it always had.

"Did you see them, Rav?" Kris called, as she and Andie emerged onto the walkway.

"Of course! I waved at them, and they waved back." But Ravi was removing the telescope from its mount, putting it back in its leather case.

"Hello, day." Kris held out her arms. "It's nice up here, isn't it? I like the feel of the day starting up."

"And not just any day," said Ravi. "It's Monday. Moon-day."

"Happy Moonday! Hey, is this the first real Moonday? It might look just the same as any other Monday, but it's not."

Kris looked over the parapet. Andie and Ravi looked too, the three of them in a row, gazing down at Chelsea Walk, and beyond it to the Thames. Andie heard the horn of a barge, the cooing of pigeons, traffic on the bridge, and a siren somewhere; she saw the leafy canopy of trees, the grass below; a dog out walking by himself, and strings of lights along the Embankment; she smelled the faintest tang of salt. It all felt fresh and brand new in the cool air of dawn.

She wanted to catch and keep this moment.

But I'll always remember, she thought, even when I'm ancient and a grandmother. The day I stood on the roof with Kris and Ravi, and watched London wake up, and there were men on the moon.

Chapter Fifteen

The Slough of Despond

"MAN ON THE MOON" dominated the news. Andie saw the same photographs again and again: the boot-print, heavily shadowed; the Earth from the moon; the two astronauts by the American flag; and Neil Armstrong reflected in Buzz Aldrin's helmet visor. The lunar module had successfully taken off from the surface and – amazingly – docked with the command module exactly as planned, and the first men on the moon were on their way back to Earth.

Andie went back to her own imagined landscapes, where the moon was silent and alone, not the focus of the world's obsessive gaze. She painted the Sea of Tranquility empty once more, with a blur of footprints, and the marks left by the spidery lunar module; beyond, the powdery surface was unmarked by humans.

On Tuesday she went with Kris to the King's Road, to deliver a batch of Marilyn's jewelry to East of the Sun, West of the Moon. She hoped Zak wouldn't be there – hadn't he said he was only helping out a friend? But he was outside, hanging T-shirts on a rail. He said, "Hi, you guys," mainly to Kris, then looked at Andie as if he recognized her from the shoplifting incident. All her family members, wherever they went, seemed to devote themselves to creating maximum embarrassment for her, Andie thought.

Kris handed over the box of jewelry to the sharp-faced blonde woman and spent a few minutes discussing which of Marilyn's pieces were selling best.

As they left the arcade, Zak, who was now at the till, said to Andie, "Tell Prue I got her message, would you? Tomorrow's cool. Quarter to nine, tell her."

"What's that about?" Kris asked, out on the pavement.

"No idea." Andie was baffled. "We went in there last week, and Prune, er, talked to Zak. I don't know what else."

"What, is she going out with him or something? That's neat."

Andie thought this most unlikely, but was reluctant to explain why. She'd cross-examine Prune about it later.

Much of the world might have been gazing at the moon, but the King's Road was still the center of its own universe: self-absorbed, inhabited by beautiful people with swishy hair and arty clothes. Where did they come from? Andie wondered. Where did they go to? Had they been bred specially from shop mannequins, or designed by the editors of *Honey*? Somehow, in the King's Road, even the plainest people, simply by being there, managed to make themselves look like the last word in cool.

Walking its length in Kris's company was at least less exhausting than with Prune, who wanted to dive into every shop and exclaim over every window display. Kris, though younger, had an air of having seen it all before, of being used to nothing else. It was Andie who wanted to stop and gaze, and who thought she glimpsed George Harrison in a passing taxi.

"It was *him*! I'm certain!"

"It wasn't!"

"It was!"

With a twinge of regret, Andie knew that she'd miss this. Slough High Street couldn't possibly match this daily parade of hipness and gorgeousness.

They were approaching the Town Hall. Standing squarely over the passers-by, the building made Andie think of a portly great-uncle with twirling mustaches, who had wandered by mistake into a disco. With its grand steps, pillared entrance and gilded clock, it looked surprised to find itself at the heart of fashion-conscious Chelsea. The gallery next door had a noticeboard outside: FASHIONS FOR THE SPACE AGE. EXHIBITION INSIDE.

"Hey, see this?" she called to Kris, who was about to walk on past.

They stopped to read. The poster gave details of a summer holiday competition, open to anyone under eighteen; entries were being displayed from now until the end of July.

"Shall we?"

"Sure, why not?"

They went inside. The gallery consisted of several rooms, one of which, light and airy, displayed the competition entries. Pictures and paintings were mounted on the walls, and on screens reaching across the middle. The work was of varying skill – some could easily have come from fashion magazines; some were clumsily drawn in colored pencil or pastel. The concept of "The Space Age" had been given wide interpretation, from spacesuits like the ones the Apollo astronauts wore, to designs inspired by Mary Quant or Biba.

"Looks like fun," Kris was saying. "You ought to have a go at this, Andie – it's not too late, is it? Why not?"

Andie stopped dead, staring. There, on a screen in front of her, were three of her own fashion drawings – mounted on card, neatly labeled, each one signed in a flourishing hand by *Prue Miller.*

"They're cool," said Kris. "See, you could do as well as that – Hey, *Prue Miller*! Is that your Prune? I didn't know she was into drawing, as well?"

"She isn't." Andie's voice came out strangled.

Kris raised her eyebrows. "They look pretty good to me."

"But they're *mine*! The ideas are hers, the clothes. *I* drew them – to cheer her up – but she never told me – the lying cow!"

Kris seemed to find this amusing. "Well, I guess you'll be letting her know what you think about that."

"You can say that again!"

"Do you think you could have your argument out on the street?" A woman's face appeared around one end of the screen, and a curly-haired toddler ducked underneath to peer at the girls, round-eyed. "Some of us are trying to enjoy the exhibition."

"Sorry." Andie hadn't realized there was someone else in the room. "But how *could* she?" she hissed at Kris. "Put *her* signature on *my* drawings! It's fraud, that's what it is!"

She stared at the drawings in indecision, half inclined to rip them off the display board. But part of her was *proud* to have work on show in an exhibition in the King's Road, even if it was just a fun summer holiday thing. The nerve of Prune, though!

"It'd be worse," Kris pointed out, "if she'd taken your paintings. Your moon pictures. I mean, these are good, but they're not really *you*, like the others are."

Andie wouldn't be pacified. It was still outrageous. It was practically *theft*.

"May as well take a look at the rest, now we're here," said Kris.

The drawings and paintings passed before Andie's eyes in a blur of color and line. She was impatient to get home, and let out the pressure that was building up inside her till she felt jet-propelled with anger and indignation.

ଓଃ

"Prune? Prune, you in?" she shouted, letting herself into the apartment.

No answer. Typical of Prune not to be around when she was wanted. Now what?

Andie ran downstairs and out to the garden, looking for Kris. And there Prune was – on the swing, swaying gently back and forth.

"Prune? What are you doing?" Andie yelled.

Prune looked up vaguely. "Waiting for Sushila."

"Oh. And then what are you doing? Going to look at the exhibition next to the Town Hall, by any chance?"

"I don't know what you're talking about," said

Prune, but the pinking of her cheeks gave her away.

"Yes, you do. Three drawings signed by *Prue Miller*. Three of *my* drawings. Signed themselves, did they? Entered themselves for the competition?"

"Oh," said Prune. "Those."

"Yes, *those*. How could you do it, Prune? How could you be so sneaky? Why didn't you *ask*?"

"They were my ideas." Prune looked at her defiantly. "You wouldn't have done it otherwise. You only did the drawing."

"*Only!* What do you mean, *only*?"

"Oh, don't be so mean, Andie! You know how much I want to work in fashion. If I win that competition—"

"If *you* win it!" Andie humphed. "Some chance! Did you look at the other entries? There are loads better than yours – I mean *mine*. How could you be so sneaky, entering my drawings with your name on them! You didn't even ask – didn't think that we could *both* have entered – didn't say a word!" She paused for breath, and relaunched. "That's just typical of you!

Whatever you want, you think you can help yourself –
like that bangle, and the Biba dress—"

"Stop it, Andie!" Prune stood up, red-faced. "Don't
keep going on at me! It was just a mistake, you know,
in the shop, and—"

"Huh! And I suppose *this* was a mistake! Signing
my pictures, and taking them to the exhibition? Don't
make me laugh—"

"What on earth's going on?"

The big male voice shocked them both into silence.
It was Patrick, standing at the top of the basement steps.

"I said what's going on? It sounds like a wild-cat-
fight's broken out. Can't you go upstairs and have
your squabble?"

He was talking in his usual mild way, but there
was a sternness behind it that made Andie feel
intimidated.

"Oh – nothing," she faltered.

"Didn't sound like nothing. What's all this about
someone signing someone else's pictures?"

Kris had come up the steps behind him. Everyone was looking at everyone else; no one was talking.

"It's – a bit complicated." Andie was first to break the silence.

"Well, cool it, will you? You're like a pair of parrots, screeching away. It's too warm inside to have the doors closed, and believe it or not, I'm trying to *work*." He turned, bumped into Kris, and went back down the steps.

"Sorry!" Andie called after him.

Kris pulled a rueful face, and followed. Prune and Andie, very aloof with each other, went up to the apartment.

As if Prune hadn't done enough already! Andie grumped to herself. Now Patrick, who she wanted so hard to impress, thought she was a squawking parrot, a raucous nuisance.

Eventually, Prune made the first move, coming into the bedroom, where Andie sat icily by the window with her sketchbook. "Listen, And. Why don't we go there, to the gallery? Then you can cross out my name and put yours, and we can ask for the entry form back and put your name on that as well."

"You go," Andie mumbled. "I can't be bothered."

Still, it was the nearest thing to *sorry* she was likely to get from Prune. And only now did she remember the message she was supposed to pass on. "I saw Zak this morning. He said fine for tomorrow, quarter to nine. What's that about? Is it a date, or what?"

"A date? No!" Prune laughed, then gave her a furtive look. "I've got a job there. I'm going to help out two days a week, Thursdays and Saturdays. Or at least I *was* – I said I'd do it for the whole summer vacation, only now how can I, when we're going back home a week from Friday?"

"Didn't you think of that?"

"Of course I did, Miss Smartypants, only I thought something would turn up. And it doesn't look like it will. We're heading back to the Slough of Despond."

Andie looked at her. "How did it happen, then,

getting the job? I mean, last time we were in there, you—"

"I know," Prune said defensively. "Tried to shoplift. You're going to say I'm the last person they'd want working there. But I liked Zak – he was funny and nice, and he didn't turn me in to Alicia – that's the manager, the woman we saw – when he easily could have. So I went back to say thank you, and – and that it *wasn't* a mistake, but I wouldn't do it again. And then he asked if I'd like to help out. I've got a job, Andie! A job in the King's Road! It's a start, isn't it?"

"I wouldn't get too excited. You'll be there three days before we go home."

ରୁ

Later, while Andie was washing the cat dishes and Mum and Dad were watching *Man Alive* on TV, Kris came up.

"Will you do me a favor? No, what I mean is, will you do yourself a favor?"

"Sure," Andie said, surprised. "What?"

"Come down and show Patrick your paintings. Your moon paintings."

Andie was suspicious. "Why?"

"Well –" Kris was unwisely trying to cuddle Rumpelteazer, who yowled, and stalked away in indignation – "I told him why you argued with Prune. And I told him about your paintings and how good they are. And he said he'd like to see them."

Andie shook her head. "No! He'll think they're rubbish."

"Up to you." Kris threw both hands up. "Have it your way. Don't bother talking to Patrick, who's – well, I'm not saying he's a genius, but he's *good,* and he makes a living from it, and he teaches students and he knows when people have got it and when they haven't, but never mind what he thinks. Go back to your dreary old art teacher, and let her tell you whether you can paint or not. Is that what you want?"

"No –"

"Right. So let's go."

Chapter Sixteen

Splashdown

Andie wished she had something better than a cardboard folder held together with string, something more likely to impress Patrick – but she needn't have worried. By the time she and Kris got down to the basement, he was nowhere to be seen.

"Oh, sorry!" Marilyn said, when they trooped back up to the kitchen, where she was slicing a pineapple. "Doug turned up unexpectedly, and they've gone to the Pheasantry to meet this record producer. Doug's his agent," she explained to Andie. "And it looks like a big contract might come out of this, so they've got a lot to talk about – I shouldn't think he'll be back till late. Oh, and you wanted to show him your pictures – what a shame!"

She sounded, Andie thought, like a kindly teacher encouraging an infant. But she didn't say that *she* wanted to see the paintings. Andie tucked the folder more firmly under her arm, wanting to hide it from view.

"Doesn't matter," she said, half-heartedly. She'd take it back upstairs where it belonged, hidden behind the armoire.

"No, leave it." Kris prised the folder from Andie's grip. "He can look tomorrow."

○3

While Andie fretted and fidgeted about not having her paintings in their usual hiding place, Prune erupted into the flat with good news.

"I can stay at Sushila's! Stay here for a whole two weeks. I needn't go back home with you!"

"What's this about?" Dad was reading the newspaper, Mum ironing one of his striped shirts.

Prune babbled it out. She was going to continue helping Mrs. Kapoor with her charity fundraising – there was a special day of speeches and talks coming up at the Town Hall in the middle of August, and Sushila was doing part of the organizing, and Prune would help, too – and she had her part-time job at East of the Sun, West of the Moon, so she'd be earning her own money, and Mr. and Mrs. Kapoor said she was welcome to stay with them, and it would be great, and Mum and Dad couldn't possibly object, could they? Not when she'd be doing something so *useful*.

"Well, I don't know." Mum was wearing her cautious expression. "I'd need to talk to the Kapoors myself. Are you sure that's what they said? And the middle of August? That's when your exam results come out. It'll be time to make decisions about your future. You'll need to be enrolled somewhere – we've put it off too long already."

"That's all right – I'll be home by then. And I've more or less decided to stay on at school, if my grades are good enough. Go on, Mum! Dad! Say yes – I want to, *so much –*"

"Well, I can't see why not, as long as—" Dad began.

"What's this about a part-time job?" Mum interrupted.

✃

Just turned midnight, and Andie was wide awake.

A week from now would be their last night at Number Six, Chelsea Walk. No more Kris. No more Ravi. No more King's Road. No more London on their doorstep, with all its excitement.

No more skywatching. Well, she could still *watch* the sky, of course; she could stand out in the back garden and look at the stars, but it wouldn't be the same without Ravi and his telescope and his knowledge. Nor would it be the same as being up high in the London rooftops, picking out landmarks.

What was she doing, lying in bed now, wasting precious time? She hadn't heard Ravi go up – no telltale creaking above her head – but he might be there, all the same.

She put on sandals and a sweater, and crept out of the apartment and up the attic stairs, tuning her ears to the silence. It was funny how silences could vary. There was the almost tingling silence when you knew something would happen, someone was there – like that first time. And then the really silent silence that meant only emptiness. The whole house was sleeping, and Andie knew, before tiptoeing past the maids' rooms and through the storeroom to the low door that led out, that Ravi wasn't there. The door was locked.

Well, he didn't come up here every night – she knew that. But all the same she felt hollow with disappointment. She went back down, and got into bed, and lay there hot and resentful as she listened to

Prune's steady breathing. Everything was working out for Prune, wasn't it? Mum and Dad had agreed that she could stay on with Sushila, and even seemed pleased at her initiative in getting the shop job. So Prune had got what she wanted, and it didn't seem at all fair, to Andie.

She thought of her worn folder, down in Patrick's apartment, and felt uneasy, wishing she hadn't left it there. First thing tomorrow, she'd go down and fetch it back.

෬

The basement doors were open. Andie went down, hearing a voice inside; but it was Marilyn, talking on the phone at her bench. There was no sign of Kris, nor of Patrick, and Andie remembered now that Kris was spending the day at a drama workshop.

"Hang on a minute." Marilyn lowered the receiver. "Have you come for your folder, Andie? It's over there." She smiled and nodded, and went back to her conversation.

The folder was lying on a drafting table on Patrick's side of the room. Andie grabbed it, and clutched it to her chest. Was that all, then? Had Patrick even bothered to look? Perhaps he had, and thought her work was awful – too childish to waste his time on.

Out in the garden, she flipped it open and had a quick look inside, thinking he might have left a note, even just a *Not bad* or a *Thank you*.

Nothing. He must think it was so awful that he couldn't think of anything to say.

❧

SPLASHDOWN DAY FOR APOLLO MOON MEN was all over today's paper; but even this excitement couldn't brighten Andie's spirits. She didn't want to look at her paintings, let alone do any more. She wandered aimlessly along the Embankment, then returned to flick aimlessly through the pages of a book. In such a slump as this, nothing seemed worth doing; with no way to cast it off, she may as well let herself wallow. There was no one around to notice, with Mum and Dad and now Prune all out at work for the day. Mungojerrie seemed delighted that she was so miserable, and lay alongside her, warm and purry. "Typical!" she told him. "You've decided you actually *like* me now, I suppose? Now that I'm nearly going home?" The Slough of Despond awaited, and maybe it was the best place for her.

Time dragged by. It was a still afternoon, the sun shining hotly through the bedroom window; it would be cooler in the garden, but Andie couldn't summon the will to move. She was annoyed with herself, but unable to do anything about it. How stupid to be wasting what little was left of her time in London!

She didn't even stir from the bed when at last a key turned in the lock of the front door.

"Come on down, And!" Prune burst into the bedroom, looking in the best of moods. One day at East of the Sun, West of the Moon, and already she looked a little less dolly-bird and a bit more Zak-like, in jeans and a patchwork vest, with a small bell on a chain round her neck.

"What's happened to you?" Andie mustered enough interest to prop herself on one elbow.

"Nothing – only everyone's down in the garden, and Patrick's opening champagne. He's got something to celebrate, he says – it's like another party!"

"Mum won't let me drink champagne," Andie grumbled, and almost added that she wasn't coming down, and had never felt less partyish, but curiosity got the better of her. She could always come back up.

Chapter Seventeen

Sparkles

Outside, everyone was sitting on deckchairs or on the grass, while Ravi had the swing. A folding table held bottles of champagne and soda, and wide glasses; Patrick was pouring, and Kris handing round the drinks.

"Well, who knows?" Patrick was saying. "You can never tell, with these rock groups – they come and go. But this bunch have really got something, in my opinion."

Mum turned around and smiled. "Oh, you're here, love. That's good."

Kris handed a glass of soda to Andie. Dad was there as well, tie loosened, suit jacket slung over the back of a deckchair. Music floated up from the basement – something electronic and spacey that sent tingles down the back of Andie's neck.

"What's going on?" she asked Kris.

"It's fantastic! Patrick's got a contract to do album covers for Legend – you know? – to give them a special look that everyone'll recognize. It's big money – the record company's really investing in them –"

"– yes, there's a feature on them in the *New Musical Express* – they're playing at the Isle of Wight next month – that's right, the rock festival – then touring the States –" Patrick was telling everyone.

"Is this them?" Andie asked Kris, meaning the music.

"Yes, aren't they fab? We'll go inside in a minute, and I'll show you the artwork. You'll love it."

In all the excitement, Kris seemed to have forgotten entirely about showing Andie's paintings to Patrick. Andie nursed a small ache of resentment that promised to swell into a rage of self-pity as soon as she was alone.

Now everyone had a glass, and Marilyn called out, "Here's to Patrick – and Legend!"

"To Patrick!"

"I'm so proud of you, darling –"

"Congratulations – well done!"

Andie took a gulp of soda, too much at once – the fizz erupted sneezily in her nose, and she doubled over, spluttering. Mum looked at her in dismay, and reached across to take the glass.

Only now, for the first time, did Patrick look at her. "Here she is! When she's quite finished choking – give her back that fizz, Maureen – we're all going to raise our glasses again, to this young lady here."

Andie recovered enough to look around the group for a young lady she couldn't have noticed, then realized with a jolt that he meant *her.*

"Andie." Patrick raised his glass to her. "You've certainly got a future as an artist, if you choose to take it. To Andie Miller, everyone – a name you're likely to hear more of –"

Kris was grinning widely. "Told you!"

"Oh! You really think so, do you?" Dad said to Patrick, looking bemused. "I always thought she was quite good – but what do I know? Art, these days – but she's never without her sketchbook and her paints –"

"She's always wanted to be an artist," Mum said doubtfully, "ever since she was little –"

"Well," said Patrick, "she *is* an artist."

Now all the faces were turned Andie's way, and it was like blinking in the beam of a spotlight.

"Are you sure?" Her voice came out as a squawk.

"Sure? I've got final-year students with less talent."

"That's very kind of you, Patrick." Mum was prim and pink, though there was no mistaking her look of pride.

"No, he's not being *kind*," Marilyn told her. "He's never kind. You should ask some of his students, the ones who crawl away in tears and shred up their work into microscopic bits. He never praises anyone's work unless he really means it."

Andie was giddy with bewilderment. "I'd love to be an art student. More than anything in the world."

"No reason why you shouldn't," Patrick said.

Andie shot a defiant look at Mum, who registered it, and explained to Patrick, "We've always encouraged her to think of it as a hobby, haven't we, Dennis? But, well –"

"There's obviously money to be made – prospects – if you know your way around," Dad said. "It doesn't have to be starving in a garret."

"There's plenty of us have done a stint of *that*, before making much progress," said Patrick. "I'm not saying it's easy – but if you've got talent, and determination – and it seems to me that Andie's got plenty of both – then good luck to you."

Now *everyone* wanted to see Andie's pictures. She had to bring them down, and suffer the embarrassment of having them looked at and exclaimed over: "That's fantastic, Andie!"..."What an imagination – I feel like I'm actually on the moon –"..."Well! We've always known she *liked* painting, and her teacher says she's got talent..."..."Talent! I should say so!" So many compliments! She thought her head would burst.

Needing to recover, she went inside with Kris to look at Patrick's artwork for the album covers.

Kris opened a portfolio – larger and smarter, as well as much fuller, than Andie's, but she didn't mind that now.

First, there was just the word LEGEND, in letters that twined through and around each other like sinuous plants.

"That's going to be their logo – it means like a trademark," Kris explained. "It'll be on the record labels, and on all their posters. They haven't decided which colors yet. And here are the sketches, and this is what they're most likely using for the first album."

Andie looked. It was a fantastical landscape – the sort of thing she might try to paint herself. Picturesque, but also faintly sinister, with towering cliffs and the black clefts of chasms, and precipitous paths, and dark forests. She imagined herself walking into it, and wondered who she might meet.

"It's kind of fairy-tale," she said at last. "Only a *serious* fairy tale."

"What's to say," said Kris, "that fairy tales can't be serious? Some of them are *very* serious."

Chapter Eighteen

We Are Stardust

On Wednesday, the Millers' last night at Chelsea Walk, Mum finally plucked up courage to invite everyone in. She had finished her agency work on Friday, and spent all Monday cleaning the apartment. Tuesday was for shopping – Andie helped – and Wednesday for packing and cooking. They prepared sausages on sticks, quiche and salads. They made egg salad and filled vol-au-vents with mushroom and ham; Mum made her specialty, lemon meringue pie.

Being so busy – even if she thought Mum was going to far more trouble than was necessary – stopped Andie from feeling too sad. All the same, several times she found herself thinking, *This is the last time. Tonight will be the last time I sleep here. The last time I live in the same house as a real artist, and Ravi and Kris. The last time I swing from the walnut tree.*

"Do you think there's enough?" When everything was ready, Mum stood back and surveyed the dining table.

"Mum! If fifteen extra people turned up, we'd *still* have enough."

Mum laughed. "It's fun, though, isn't it? I know I get myself too wound up, but I *like* this. We ought to do it more often, have people round. People at home, I mean. They've been so friendly, haven't they, Patrick and Marilyn and the Kapoors? I hope you're not too disappointed, Andie, this not working out."

Sometimes Andie felt that Mum was too busy

fussing to take proper notice of her; but now Mum had stopped folding napkins, and was looking at her very seriously.

"Well, a bit," Andie said. "But there are nice things about going back home. There's Barbara, and not having to share with Prune. Even not having to change schools."

"I know. I like it here, but I'm looking forward to being back in our own home. But it hasn't been a wasted summer for you here, has it? Making friends with Kris and Ravi, and Patrick thinking so highly of you. He obviously knows what he's talking about. The thing is, me and Dad don't know anything about painting and art. It's another world, to us. But we shouldn't stand in your way, if that's where you want to go. We were talking about it last night. We're very proud of you."

She gave Andie a hug. Automatically, Andie wriggled away; she managed a gruff, "Thanks, Mum. That's great."

Had Mum really said that? What was going on – everyone saying such nice things? Andie thought of Patrick's words as fantastic shiny presents which she could keep unwrapping over and over again.

Wasted summer? How could it have been? Not only had an artist – a real artist – admired her work, but these few weeks had shown her the moon and the stars, the immensity and the mystery. The wonder. And she would always have that, whenever she looked up at the sky on a clear night.

CB

It wasn't as if she was losing her new friends, either. "Slough isn't a million miles away," Ravi had said. "You can come up on the train, can't you? We'll go to the Science Museum again, and the Planetarium, and Madame Tussaud's, and the Geological Museum, and the Zoo."

"Come on a Saturday, and we'll all go see a film," added Kris.

And Prune would be here for another two weeks.

Now that they were going to be separated, Andie felt – rather to her own surprise – that she would actually *miss* Prune.

"Prune? If you want to do any more fashion designs, I don't mind drawing them for you," she offered. "As long as – you know."

"Thanks," said Prune, "but I'm going to be a bit busy for now, with my job and everything. Still, that's nice of you." After a moment, she added: "Do you think you could stop calling me Prune now? You know I don't like it."

This seemed fair enough; Andie agreed. "It'll be hard. But I'll try."

ॐ

Ravi had spent the last two weeks making a cassette tape of all the songs he could find that were about space or the moon, and it was playing now: "Bad Moon Rising," "Space Oddity," "In the Year 2525." As usual, the grown-ups ate and drank and chatted, but there was only one thing Andie really wanted to do.

As soon as it was dark enough, Ravi fetched his telescope, and he, Kris and Andie went up to the roof. *One last time,* went through Andie's head like a refrain, as they climbed the narrow stairs and went through the storeroom and out.

There it was, the moon. Alone again. Pale, almost transparent, above the glow of London. But of course it wasn't really transparent. It was a place.

"It's still hard to believe, isn't it?"

They were taking turns with the telescope.

"From now on," said Andie, "it'll be Dad's binoculars in the back garden. But at least I've got my skymarks."

"Your dad's binoculars are probably as powerful as Galileo's telescope," said Ravi. "And with that he saw the moons of Jupiter."

"What would he have thought of people flying to the moon?" Kris wondered.

"What would my great-grandmother have thought?" said Ravi. "When she came from India,

Queen Victoria was still alive and there were horse-drawn carriages in the streets. But that's like a split second ago, when you think of stars shining at us from hundreds of thousands of light years away."

"It makes us seem so tiny and unimportant," said Andie. "Like specks of dust."

"We *are* specks of dust," Ravi told her. "That's what we're made of. Stardust."

"Oh! You mean, like in the 'Woodstock' song?" Kris started to sing it, in a warbling voice.

"That's right! We've got to be made of the same stuff as stars – whatever it was that exploded when the universe began. Because what else *is* there for us to be made of?"

"But – all of this?" Andie stretched out her hands – to the street below, the traffic, the Albert Bridge, to the rest of London on the other side of the river.

"Everything. Everything there is. The same beginning," said Ravi. Then he clapped his hands over his ears and turned on Kris, who was pulling a contorted face as she strained for the highest notes. "Is someone strangling a hyena? You're making my brain hurt!"

"See, Andie?" Kris broke off singing. "You don't have to want to be a star, with your painting. You *are* one, already. We all are."

Andie had been about to say, "It's impossible! Everything made of stars?"

But *lots* of things seemed impossible, and not all of them were. Humans had been to the moon, and left footprints, and come back again. There were two people alive who had stood on another world.

If that was possible, who could say what wasn't?

☙

Glossary

&

Chelsea Girl – this was a popular chain of low-price fashion shops

Aga – a type of large iron oven

cricket – a bat-and-ball sport that originated in England, played by two opposing teams

Enid Blyton – a prolific English children's author who wrote some of her most famous stories (including the *Famous Five* and *Secret Seven* series) between the 1940s and 1960s. Her *Malory Towers* stories were set at a private boarding school

Jean Shrimpton – an iconic English supermodel in the 1960s. Her nickname was "The Shrimp"

O-Levels – the "O" stands for "ordinary". These were the standard exams from the 1950s to the 1980s, which schoolchildren had to take around the age of 15

pounds, shillings, crowns, half-crowns and pence – the pound was (and still is) the basic unit of currency in England, and there are now 100 pence (pennies) in a pound. The others are all coins that used to be part of the currency: Before 1971, the pound was divided into twenty shillings and there were twelve pence in a shilling (so 240 pennies in a pound). A crown was worth five shillings (a quarter of a pound), and a half-crown was worth two-shillings-and-sixpence (an eighth of a pound).

Twiggy – (born Lesley Hornby) another iconic English supermodel of the 1960s, who still works as a model today. She was given the nickname Twiggy because of her thin build

Author's note

Having so much enjoyed writing *Polly's March*, my first Historical House novel, I was delighted to have the chance to return to Number Six, Chelsea Walk, this time for the summer of 1969. Not only was this the time of the Apollo 11 mission, the first moon landing, but it was the era of "Swinging London," an eruption of young fashion and music and hipness – and Chelsea, especially the King's Road, was at the heart of all this.

I always enjoy researching, and never more than for *Andie's Moon*. I spent a lot of time gazing at the moon and trying to find my way around the night sky; I watched and watched the TV coverage of Neil Armstrong and Buzz Aldrin on the lunar surface, and listened to Armstrong's famous words; I visited the Science Museum, meeting a curator, John Liffen, who was actually there on the day of the Apollo launch, and told me how people gathered to watch the live broadcast from Cape Kennedy. And then there was the fashion and the music. Twiggy, Biba, Simon and

Garfunkel, *The Stones in the Park* – these names alone conjure the freshness and excitement of the time. I hope *Andie's Moon* will transport you to the 1960s. Even, maybe, to the moon...

Linda Newbery

About the author

Linda Newbery is the successful author of over twenty books for children and teenagers. She was first inspired to write when teaching English at a high school. Her novels have garnered much critical acclaim, including *Set in Stone*, which won a prestigious UK children's book award.

Linda lives with her husband and four cats in Northamptonshire, England.

To find out more about Linda Newbery, you can visit her website: www.lindanewbery.co.uk.

Usborne Quicklinks

For links to interesting websites where you can see Sixties fashions, watch video clips of the first moon landing and go "sky hopping", go to the Usborne Quicklinks Website at www.usborne-quicklinks.com and enter the keywords "andie's moon".

Internet safety

When using the Internet, make sure you follow these safety guidelines:

- Ask an adult's permission before using the Internet.
- Never give out personal information, such as your name, address or telephone number.
- If a website asks you to type in your name or e-mail address, check with an adult first.
- If you receive an e-mail from someone you don't know, don't reply to it.

Usborne Publishing is not responsible and does not accept liability for the availability or content of any website other than its own, or for any exposure to harmful, offensive, or inaccurate material which may appear on the Web. Usborne Publishing will have no liability for any damage or loss caused by viruses that may be downloaded as a result of browsing the sites it recommends. We recommend that children are supervised while on the Internet.